I0823549

This Ain't Our First Rodeo

This Ain't Our First Rodeo

BY LIARA TAMANI

Greenwillow Books
An Imprint of HarperCollins*Publishers*

HarperCollins Children's Books, a division of HarperCollins Publishers,
195 Broadway, New York, NY 10007

HarperCollins Publishers,
Macken House, 39/40 Mayor Street Upper, Dublin 1, D01 C9W8, Ireland

Greenwillow Books is an imprint of HarperCollins Publishers.

This Ain't Our First Rodeo

harpercollins.com

ISBN 978-0-06-309333-1

The text of this book is set in Director's Cut Pro.
Book design by Sylvie Le Floc'h.
25 26 27 28 29 LBC 5 4 3 2 1
First Edition

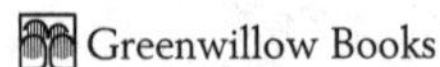

To Mommy, Daddy,
and Houston, Texas—thank you
for raising me with grit and grace. I love you!

This Ain't Our First Rodeo

Shawn

I can't help thinking about how things could go left. Dad could get thrown off and trampled to death. The bull could crack his skull. Crush his ribs. Or toss him in the air and send a horn through his chin again.

Things I never allow myself to think about when I'm the one in the bucking chute. No time for that. Gotta block everything out and secure my grip. Because when that gate flies open, it's me against a fifteen-hundred-plus-pound beast. Can't beat a bull on strength, though. Gotta flow with him. Nothing like linking with horses, but I always find a way to hold on. Eight seconds minimum, but I aim for ten to make sure I win.

But tonight ain't about me.

It's Dad's final ride in his last rodeo. After nineteen years in the game, he's going out with a bang. RodeoHouston, the largest rodeo in the world. Twenty days of steer wrestling, barrel racing, bareback riding, all kinds of roping, and of course the main event—bull riding. Two and a half million people roll through every year to see us cowboys and cowgirls do our thang.

Dad gives the nod. He's good to go. Smoking Hot, a two-thousand-pounder with a reputation for doing whatever it takes to get riders on the ground, is staring out of the gate like he's ready too. There's a camera in Dad's face and bright lights flashing all around.

"You got this, Dad!" I scream from the back side of the bucking chute.

They're out of the gate. Smoking Hot starts spinning right away.

"Keep riding!" I shout.

The bull twists and kicks, trying to buck him off, but Dad ain't going nowhere.

"That's right! Hold tight!"

Seven seconds in.

"Yeah!"

Eight seconds! My dad made the whistle on Smoking Hot. Did what so many other riders have found impossible.

"Yeah, yeah, yeah! That's what I'm talking about!" I scream over fifty thousand fans.

But right after Dad dismounts, Smoking Hot bucks again and knocks him to the ground. The beast kicks, and his hind legs come down right beside Dad's head.

A cold front sweeps through my body, freezing everything.

Then a bullfighter steps in and runs off in the opposite direction. A chase that allows Dad to hop up.

Thank God.

Over the loudspeakers, the announcer says, "Sterling Williams, ladies and gentlemen! A five-time PBR world finalist right here from Houston, Texas!"

Dad runs to the section where my stepmom, Shelly, and two sisters are sitting, climbs to the top rung of the gate, and blows them a kiss. Now Shelly is on the Jumbotron in tears. The whole arena rises to their feet to show Dad love.

"That's right! Give it up for Sterling's dominating performance tonight," the announcer continues. "And here come the numbers. Eighty-eight points! Sliding his way into the top two. What a way to end a magnificent career!"

I can't believe I just watched Dad's last pro ride. For so long, I've been his biggest fan. But he says it's his turn to be mine now.

Dad's been putting me in bull-riding competitions since I was ten. And now he's talking like I can be the best bull rider in the world. Get my name into the hall of fame like Charlie Sampson or Myrtis Dightman.

It's hard to imagine. But I can't lie, it feels good making him so proud. Too bad I won't be able to ride around the hood with my boys as much. But Dad says there's no more time for playing around on horses. Gotta get serious about bull riding so I'm ready to go pro as soon as I turn eighteen.

Only two more years.

Josie

He's my last chance. The boy in the leather puffer vest, on the other side of the caviar bar, sneaking a sip of his mom's champagne. A sign that he can't be trusted? Probably, but it's not like I'm looking for a boyfriend.

His mom is busy posing with the ten-foot-tall glittering gold horse, which is dutifully wearing a black bandana that reads *Riley Ranch*. Now his dad is showing his mom the pictures he took. Nope. Not cute enough.

The boy tries his dad's amber-colored drink and makes a face—nasty.

A slight tilt of her cowboy hat and a quick finger comb of her long blond braids before taking more pics. Still a no-go.

Another sip of the champagne.

More pics.

Another sip.

More pics.

A line is forming for the gold rhinestone horse, and his dad appears done with playing photographer. Last sip and the boy hands the drinks back to his parents without them noticing a thing—too slick for his own damn good.

But who am I to judge? His parents seem to be just like mine. In their own world. Not paying him any mind. They've already turned away from him to schmooze with the news lady and her husband, who are dressed as a saloon girl and sheriff. Clearly, they knew the assignment. We're in the saloon. The steakhouse stopped seating guests ten minutes ago.

The boy hasn't seen me yet. I'm sitting in the corner on a velvet tufted sofa, waiting for the perfect moment to approach him. "Ouch," I moan, and tug at the sequined jacket that Mom made me put on. I've somehow ripped the satin lining in the armpit and the stupid little sequins keep reaching through and clawing at me.

Makes me wish I could take this fancy thing off and toss it onto the two-tiered antler chandelier overhead. Bet I could land it my first try. But Mom would kill me if I took this jacket off. Apparently, my tank top, cutoff jean shorts, cowboy hat, and boots aren't good enough. Even at the rodeo!

I swear, when my parents said they were opening a restaurant at the rodeo called Riley Ranch, I thought Mimi and Papa's ranch would be the inspiration. Leave it to my parents to set up a tent in the parking lot of a stadium filled with livestock and give it lacquered walls, wooden beams, chandeliers, gold-framed paintings, mirrors, and marble bars. It's just as fancy as their other Houston restaurants: Riley Chateau, Riley Ristorante, Riley Cove, and Riley Steakhouse. All different with the same family brand that, according to our website, promises a swanky design, five-star flavor, and a see-and-be-seen atmosphere.

Now back to the boy. One of those light-eyed, light-skinned, curly-hair types—a little too pretty if you ask me. Downright obnoxious when you add the smug smirk he's wearing. Look at him over there pretending to check the time on his diamond-encrusted watch even though he has a phone in his hands. So dumb. But the type of boy Mom would probably love for me to hang out with.

I get up and walk toward him.

When he notices me approaching, he looks confused and then scared, like he thinks he's in trouble.

So I decide to put the fancy jacket and my height to good use and play with him a bit. Lowering the brim of my hat, I say, "This establishment has a strict policy on underage drinking, young man," in the most adult voice I can muster.

Greenish-brown eyes looking terrified, he says, "I didn't. I swear I didn't—"

"We have a holding cell around back and the sheriff has requested that I escort you out there for the rest of the night."

"What?" he whines. "I didn't even do anything."

"I'm kidding," I tell him, so I don't end up making his scary butt cry.

He lets out a deep breath.

"Come on, I'm only fifteen," I confess.

He doesn't say anything. Only stares at me.

"Sorry, I was just having a little fun." I extend my hand. "Hi, I'm Josie."

"Reggie," he says, his grip weak.

It feels gross, and I let go. "Have you been to the carnival yet?" I ask, getting to the point. I wish my cousin Billie were here to go with me, but her spring break isn't until next week.

"No," he says, looking confused.

"It closes at midnight. We could go and be back before this place shuts at one."

Now he's looking at me like I'm a crazy person. "We, as in me and you?"

"It's not like that. My parents won't let me go alone," I explain, glancing toward them through the archway to the steakhouse. They're talking to a couple and gesturing to the painting of a girl and boy sitting on a horse, facing each other, against a backdrop of land and sky. I was hoping they wouldn't sell that one. Save it for me. But I guess I never wrote the proposal Daddy asked for. I swear he wants a stupid proposal for everything. So annoying.

"Basically, you want to use me?" Reggie asks.

"Well, I wouldn't put it like that."

"Of course you wouldn't. Not a pretty girl like you."

I never understood boys who like to belittle girls out of one side of their mouths while complimenting us out of the other. Seriously, what's the point? Do they enjoy giving off slimy, patronizing vibes, or do they think we're just too dumb to notice? I want to tell him, *Boy, bye*. But it's the last night of the rodeo and I still haven't been to the carnival. So I ask, "Don't you want to get on some rides?"

"Not really. I just got here. Plus, I haven't even seen any celebrities yet."

"Come on, please," I say, hating myself for begging.

"What's in it for me?" he asks, and looks me up and down hungrily.

I roll my eyes. This is exactly why I don't deal with boys.

They're gross. And to think when I was younger, I couldn't wait to fall in love. Love seemed to be all around—in the country songs Papa played on his banjo, in the R&B music Mom sang along to in the car, in movies, in the good morning and goodbye kisses my parents and grandparents shared all the time. And I waited for it, arms wide open, like I do every time I see a butterfly, hoping it would land on me too.

"Or I can just stay here," he says.

Doesn't help that most of the boys I'm around are accustomed to getting whatever they want. Or, like me, have probably listened to one too many negotiating strategies. But everything in life can't be a transaction. "Fine, 50 Cent is over there," I offer up reluctantly.

His eyes widen. "What? Where?"

"On the other side of the bar, beside the neck mount."

"The what?"

"The deer head sticking out of the wall. I can introduce you if you want."

"For real?"

"Yeah, he comes into my parents' restaurants all the time."

"Yo, I can't believe this. Wait till I tell the homies!" he says, staring at 50.

"But you have to be cool if I take you over there," I say, thinking about the fact that I'm about to break one of my parents' restaurant rules: never bother celebrities. Usually not a problem for me because I could care less about famous people.

"Yeah, yeah. I'll be cool."

"Then afterward, you'll go to the carnival with me?" I ask.

"Yeah, yeah, yeah. No doubt. We can ride all the rides. Whatever you want."

Do I even have to tell you that sneaking, lying, slimy Reggie didn't keep his word? After he got a selfie and one-armed hug from 50, he got on his phone and said he was busy.

I look around for my parents again. Spot Daddy walking hurriedly into the kitchen. Mom air-kissing the cheeks of some lady in red leather pants. Going off opening night, they both should be busy until at least two a.m.

Keeping my eyes on Mom, I slowly get up and make my way toward the exit. She's wearing a blue sequined dress that almost looks like denim, a custom hat to match, and a sash that says *Riley Ranch Rodeo Queen*. Exactly the future she wants for me.

But I'm no princess.

Regardless of what my parents think, I can handle myself. I'll be fine. Back to sitting pretty in their version of a ranch before they realize I'm gone.

Shawn

What emotions are running through you right now? Can you talk about the mental and physical toughness it takes to be a professional bull rider for nineteen years? What will you miss most? How do you plan to transition from the adrenaline rush of bull riding to everyday life?

Dad loves the cameras. I don't. So before these reporters get any ideas about getting a two-for-one, I'm out. I'll text Dad and Shelly to let them know that I went to the carnival. Shelly already left to get the girls into bed, anyway, so I know she won't care. Can't leave the rodeo without hopping on my favorite ride again. The best Ferris wheel in Houston only comes around once a year.

Josie

As soon as I step out of the tent and see the brightly lit food vendors with Texas-sized corn dogs, funnel cakes, and deep-fried cookies and candy bars, my mouth starts watering. Love me some carnival food, but I tell my taste buds to hold their horses. Fun first.

Starting with the Ferris wheel. Towering above everything, it'll be a good way to get a lay of the land—best rides, shortest lines, and games that aren't rigged.

Heading toward the gigantic, revolving circle glowing with blinking purple lights, I get another poke under the arm. Off with this stupid jacket, and I start tying it around my waist. Hard to do in this herd of people all dressed up in the western gear they probably only pull out once a year, but I finally get it done.

I'll barely have any time for rides if I stay in this crowd. So I make a quick left between Buttermilk Bacon on a Stick and Crawfish Cowboy—through wires, generators, and smoky deep fryers—to an alley behind the vendors. I can follow the fence all the way around to the Ferris wheel. Probably longer, but it'll be so much quicker because no one is back here.

I swear I love how smart I am sometimes.

Shawn

Where is she going? I wonder, looking at the girl in a cowboy hat and shiny silver skirt, strutting like nobody's business on the other side of the chain link fence.

And just like that, she's out of view.

I'm taking a shortcut through the field of stock trailers. Don't ask me why, but I hook a quick left between a row of them, even though the carnival entrance is in the opposite direction.

She passes under a light post, and I glimpse the glittering fringe swinging from her skirt and her strong, long legs. Man, this girl is booking it.

I cut through the trailers again and accidentally startle two horses, staring at me through the bars of an open-top trailer, eyes wide with fear. Couldn't see me coming in the dark. "My bad," I tell them.

I don't see the girl at all this time.

I speed up.

Only a boot.

I walk even faster, hunching between trailers, trying not to surprise any more livestock.

Hold up, she's not alone anymore. Some dude in a bright yellow baseball cap is approaching her. Can't place it, but I've seen that hat somewhere else today.

Anyway, the girl isn't interested. She keeps it moving and tries to sidestep him. But he blocks her path. So she tries to walk around him the other way.

I run to the next aisle.

They're not there.

I run back.

He's all up in her face.

A knot starts forming in my chest—same one I get every time I climb onto the back of a bull—and I take off in a full sprint.

Josie

"Don't touch me," I say after the boy in the smiley face hat grabs one of the sequined sleeves tied around my waist and runs his hand up it.

"I was just seeing if your jacket flips like those pillows do in Target."

I'm about to explain that the jacket is on my body, not some shelf in a store, when I remember I'm not talking to a two-year-old. "Excuse me," I say, and try to get around him again.

He steps in front of me. "You're not being very nice, you know."

"Get out of my way," I say, sizing him up. He's not that much bigger or taller than me. I could probably take him.

"Okay. But first, you need to pay the toll," he says, and tugs at a piece of fringe hanging from my jacket.

I shove him in the chest. "I said don't touch me."

He barely moves and laughs. "Oh, I see I have a tough girl on my hands." He pushes me back with a force that sends me flying to the concrete.

Ouch! Right hip and shoulder throbbing, I quickly try to get up, struggling not to show how much it hurt.

But he walks directly over me and stops, looking down

with black eyes and a nasty smirk.

"Back off!" I yell. When he doesn't, I try to punch him where I know it'll hurt.

He catches my fist and twists my wrist.

"Ow," I let slip, and yank my hand back. I look around, wishing I was on the other side of the food trucks with the rest of the crowd. I think about yelling for help, but the generators and carnival rides are so loud. So I briefly close my eyes and pray that God is looking and will save me somehow.

"Ain't so tough now, are you?" he says, and knocks the hat off my head.

A dark thunderstorm erupts in my chest—hopelessness howling, rage flashing, and fear coming down in sheets. A heavy cloud travels up my face. But I grit my teeth, determined not to shed a tear.

"Leave her alone!" a voice calls from the other side of the fence. Then a tall boy in a cowboy hat and boots scales the fence like it's nothing and hops down. Swings on the creep, no questions asked. Hits him right in the nose and knocks him to the ground.

Shocked, I just sit there and stare.

A hand reaches out to me. Pulls me up. "You okay?"

I nod, shaking from all the anger and fear still coursing through my veins.

He steps past me to pick up my hat. Dusts it off and gives it back before returning his attention to the boy still on the ground.

I want to go over there and kick that stupid boy in the

ribs. Or maybe stomp his face with my heel. At least snatch that dumb smiley face hat off his head and chuck it in the trash. But I'm so riled up I can't even move. Can't give him the middle finger or yell, *Fuck you!*

Shawn

"What the hell is your problem?" I say, standing over Donny.

"I was just playing around with her," he says, crab walking away from me.

I've known Donny since we were kids and have fought him more than a few times over the years. Fool stays starting stuff. It's like he can't help himself. Whether it's fighting, gambling, stealing, or harassing somebody, dude is gonna find some nonsense to get into.

Apple don't fall far from the tree. His dad is an illegal bookie on the rodeo circuit. You know, for fans seeking their own adrenaline rush. "Well, next time you feel like playing around with somebody, come find me," I tell him.

Now he's up on his feet, backing away even faster. When he gets two food trucks away, he yells, "I'ma see you, Shawn!" and takes off running.

I turn back to the girl. "You sure you're okay?"

Arms folded across her chest, she nods again.

"Are you hurt?"

She shakes her head no. She's a tall girl. Probably about as tall as Mom was. Five nine, five ten. And she has that natural beauty. Flawless brown skin, high cheekbones, fresh-out-of-twist long hair, and big eyes with thick lashes that look like her own.

"Do you have your phone? Is there anyone you want to call?"

She shakes her head no again and tightens the jacket around her waist before refolding her arms.

"Sorry about your jacket," I say, eyeing silver bits all over the ground. There's a big patch of the shiny stuff missing from the area covering her hip. "I'm Shawn," I say, and extend my hand.

She doesn't speak or unfold her arms. A little rude, but I get it, considering what Donny just put her through.

Josie

It's over, I try to tell myself. *I'm safe*. But my body won't listen. My heart is beating so hard it's about to burst out of my chest. And everything inside me is still flashing red.

"Sorry you had to go through that," the boy continues. "I'm glad I was back here. He must've lost his mind putting his hands on a girl like that."

"Girl? Would it have mattered if I was a boy?" I finally explode, pissed at how powerless I felt. Like a stupid damsel in distress. That's not who I am! But in that moment, it was. And there wasn't a damn thing I could do about it. Makes me so mad I could cry. But there's no way I'm about to let that happen.

"Yeah," he says, as if it's a dumb question.

"Really? How so?" I ask, determined to win this fight.

"I don't know. I probably wouldn't have noticed you if you were a dude. But even if I had, I wouldn't have been as concerned. Girls are different."

I swear he sounds just like Mom. I can hear her now—*It's all fun and games out there riding your horse, but ranch work is not suitable for girls. Do you really want to be mucking stalls and checking water troughs in the Texas heat all day? How about dealing with maggots in feed bins?*

Or swarms of biting flies? And for what? To barely cover expenses and not be able to afford nice things? I didn't escape that life only to have my daughter return to it—and I roll my eyes.

Shawn

I must've struck some type of nerve with this girl. But I don't want to argue, so I smile and try to lighten her mood with a joke. "Is this how you always treat the people who rescue you?"

She doesn't think it's funny. "Rescue? You can't be serious."

"I'm playing," I tell her, still smiling.

"Clearly not."

"I was. I swear."

"What's next? Swearing on your mother's grave? How old are you? Five?"

I stop smiling. There's only so much I can take. "Like I said, I was playing, but I can get serious if you want me to."

"Go ahead, then," she says, and cocks her head to the side.

"Well, you weren't in the best situation. And I did help you out," I say, trying to stay cool.

She laughs under her breath and shoots me a disgusted look. "So what, you're supposed to be my hero now?"

This girl is something else. Must think she's too good for a simple *thank you*. Nah, she'd rather argue, insult me, and bring Mom—God bless her soul—into this instead. I should've known when I picked up her hat and saw that it was a real Stetson Diamante that she'd be some kind of spoiled rich girl. "You said it. Not me," I finally respond.

Glaring at me, she flips her long, wavy hair and says, "Well, I can be my own hero. Thank you very much." Then she unties her jacket, tosses it over her shoulder, and struts off toward the crowd.

Man, this girl is a piece of work, but I still hate to think of her walking around the carnival by herself. I can almost hear Dad's voice telling me to never let a girl walk alone at night. Always walk them to their door and wait until they're safely inside before taking off.

But this is different. We're in public. And I don't even know this girl. She's not my responsibility.

So why is it killing me to watch her get farther away?

She pauses in between the two food trucks, and I foolishly hold out hope that she'll turn around and apologize. Instead, she balls up her fancy jacket and throws it in the trash. Keeps walking toward the crowd without looking back.

Almost involuntarily, I yell, "Wait! Where are you going? At least let me walk you to your people."

Man, I'll tell you. Sometimes, I hate the way I was raised.

Josie

Most boys would've already called me their worst and been on their way. Surprised that he's still here, offering to help, I can feel the alarm system blaring inside my body quiet down. My stubbornness still wants to tell him that I don't need a bodyguard. But honestly, after what just happened, I don't want to be by myself.

Feeling a mixture of thankfulness and suspicion, I stop and turn around.

He's already coming toward me.

Calmer, I can see that he doesn't look dressed up in rodeo clothes like everyone else. His slow stride and broad shoulders look natural in his boots, hat, white tee, big buckle, and jeans. Like a true cowboy.

When he finally catches up, he asks, "Where do you need to go?"

Wait, I think, staring at his glowing brown skin, the way his lashes curl back to kiss his lids, his full lips, and the small scar on his chin—the perfect touch of ruggedness. *How did I miss how beautiful this boy is?*

Usually the worst kind.

I search his eyes for something hidden, something he might want in return, but they seem genuine.

"Did you come here with your parents?" he asks.

I stare at him in disbelief. His kindness, even after I popped off, feels as rare as a double rainbow after a storm.

"Your friends?"

Sorry, I want to tell him. *I didn't mean to go off, at least not on you.* I look deep into his dark brown eyes, trying to come up with the right words to explain myself. But it's taking too long and beginning to feel weird. So I ask, "Would you mind getting on some rides first?"

"Fine," he says coolly.

But his willingness sends a rush of warmth through my chest. "Thanks. Can we start with the Ferris wheel?"

"Sure," he repeats in the same cold way.

Another flash of heat.

As we make our way through the thick crowd, he looks back at me every ten seconds or so to make sure I'm still here.

Yes, my whole heart lit.

Shawn

I'm on top of the world! And from up here, it looks so bright. To my right, loud colors shoot from carnival rides, food trucks, and the stadium in the background. To my left, headlights move through parking lots and zip along the freeway. At the edges, in all directions, a sea of city lights stretches to meet the sky. And don't even get me started on the moon. Not quite full yet, but still out here stunting on everybody. Man, this never gets old.

"Have you ever been on a Ferris wheel?" the girl asks, breaking the silence. We're alone in the enclosed glass cabin, and she's sitting next to me even though there's an empty bench on the other side.

"Yeah, who hasn't?" I answer, wondering what else she thinks she knows about me.

"I don't know. I'm sure lots of people," she says, staring at me.

I keep my mouth shut and look past her at the rides below.

"Not everyone has been to a carnival before."

I want her to be wrong, but then I think about some of the dudes in my neighborhood and know she isn't. Still, I say, "Well, I have."

She ignores my attitude. "I just asked because your face . . . It looked so . . . happy."

No way I'm telling her that the Ferris wheel is my all-time favorite ride. That I've ridden it both weekends and all of spring break. So that's ten times at this rodeo alone. And if I count all the rodeo carnivals I've been to over the last year, we're probably talking at least a hundred spins in the sky.

"It's nice being up here, isn't it?" she says.

"Yeah," I finally respond, still avoiding her eyes.

"What do you want to ride next?"

"It's whatever," I answer, and keep looking beyond her at the carnival. We're lower now, three pods from getting off.

"Oh my gosh. I've just realized you don't even know my name. How rude could I possibly be?"

Very, I think.

"I'm Josie," she says, still staring.

I don't want to look at her, I really don't. But I can't be out here not making eye contact during an introduction. That's weak. "Shawn," I say, finally allowing my eyes to meet hers.

"Yeah, I remember."

I nod and try to tear myself away from her gaze. But her eyes are like magnets, pulling me in. *Nah.* I force myself to look at the world beyond her. As pretty as she is, I don't have time to be dealing with stuck-up girls. I'll make sure she gets back to her people safely. But until then, I'm good on all the eye-gazing and conversation.

Josie

Up in the air with him, I had the perfect chance to apologize. But I wasn't ready to rewatch myself so scared and weak and mean, so I let it go. And now we're walking through the crowd again.

Each time he looks back to check on me, I think, *Sorry*, hoping it'll show. But clearly it's not enough.

There's no line for Alien Abduction. Inside the rotating vessel, our bodies are forced against the slanted wall while we spin with our feet dangling. I love it. It's like being out of control and having someone hold you and keep you safe at the same time. Even though I'm dizzy when we get off, I say, "Again, again!"

Shawn looks a little sick. "You can. I'll wait out here."

When I get off the ride, Shawn is talking to some glammed-up girl in an embroidered western shirt, looking just as comfortable in her rodeo clothes as he does. The way she touches his arm as she laughs makes my upper lip hike up.

I'm fully aware that Shawn is not mine. I've literally known the boy for less than an hour. But that doesn't stop me from wanting to tell Cowgirl Barbie to back off. I just hope she's not his girlfriend. "Hey, I'm Josie," I say, walking up and extending my hand.

"Tara," she says with a decent grip.

I'm instantly jealous of her smooth callouses. I can't ride Strawberry often enough for callouses to form except for in the summertime. So all week, I've been nursing nasty blisters. Mimi and Papa keep telling me to be light on the hands, but it's hard when I barely get to practice. "You ride?" I ask.

She lifts her perfectly shaped brows. "Yeah, you?"

"Yep," I answer.

"Strange we haven't run into each other. How old are you?"

"Fifteen."

"Sixteen. You competing at BPIR in Dallas next month?" she asks, referring to the Bill Picket Invitational Rodeo. A rodeo that features black cowboys and cowgirls from around the country. Mimi and Papa have pictures from the years they competed in it and other rodeos in albums alongside sepia photos of distant relatives on horseback, in wagons, and posing stone-faced in hats, chaps, and bell-skirted dresses.

"Oh, I don't compete," I say. "I love horses, though. I want to be a trainer."

"My mom was a horse trainer. Not enough action for me," she says, and looks at Shawn shamelessly.

Not knowing whether to feel more attacked by the shade or the nastiness, I ask, "What events do you compete in?"

"Mostly breakaway roping and barrel racing these days."

"You any good?" I ask, only half kidding.

"I'm okay," she says.

"If you don't get on somewhere with that," Shawn joins in playfully. Then he looks at me and says, "This girl is one of the best junior barrel racers in the country. Hands down."

Well, hello there, I think, staring at his dark eyes and broad grin—a dangerously cute combo. It's good to see him being himself.

Tara gives him a flirtatious one-armed shove and comes back with, "Yeah, says the junior bull-riding champion of the world for the last three years." Then she turns to me. "Shawn is lightweight famous, if you didn't know."

I fake smile, staring at the lash peeling from the outside corner of her right eye. I think about giving her a hint that she needs to fix it but don't.

"Whatever," Shawn says, and laughs.

"And don't even get me started on you and your little horse crew all over the internet," she says before turning back to me. "They have a name and everything: 44 Cowboys."

"That's just me and my friends having a little fun," Shawn says, and tilts his hat over his face.

Oh my goodness. Embarrassed Shawn just might be my favorite version of him yet.

"Oh, who's acting modest now?" Tara says before suddenly wiping the smile off her face and turning her attention to an older-looking boy in all denim. He's walking toward us with a funnel cake.

The mound of powdered sugar on top of the squiggly fried dough makes my mouth water. All it needs is some strawberries.

"Oh, my boyfriend is here. I gotta go," she says, and

rushes off before the poor guy has a chance to join us.

As she walks away, I eye the embroidered cherries on the back pockets of her tight jeans—pretty much an open invitation for everyone, including Shawn, to check out her butt—hating how cute they are.

Shawn

"Y'all used to date?" Josie asks.

Now that it's just us, part of me wants to remember how rude she was. But it's hard to stay mad at a pretty girl who loves horses. "Tara and me? Nah, she would chew me up and spit me out."

Josie looks at me skeptically, as if she thinks there's more to the story.

"What?"

"That funnel cake looked good, didn't it?"

Now, she knows that's not what she was thinking. But I let us both off the hook and say, "I don't eat doughnut intestines."

Cracks her up. "Oh my gosh. Entirely too accurate. You're wrong for that."

I love her laugh. High-pitched with the cutest dimples. Would've been a shame to have missed it.

"Don't tell me you're one of those weird don't-like-sweets kind of people?" she asks, eyes holding mine.

I don't even try to resist. "Nah, just more of a chocolate person."

"Humph, well, have you ever had a deep-fried candy bar?"

"Now why would I want to eat a stick of diabetes?"

"Boy, shut up," she says, and laughs. "Trust me, you're going to love it." And before I know it, she's taking my hand and pulling me back into the crowd.

Catches me off guard at first, and I don't register the moisture and swollenness of her upper palm right away. But when my brain finally gets hold of my body and lets it know that I'm not in sixth grade anymore, that I've held plenty of girls' hands before, I feel the blisters. Hoping I haven't hurt her, I loosen my grip.

Josie must think I'm trying to let go because she holds my hand tighter. Then she looks back at me over her shoulder and says, "It's better this way."

She ain't lying. We're slicing through the crowd, Josie leading me this way and that. Not the usual position I find myself in. But I can't even lie, I love how strong and confident she is.

She finds a food truck without a line, Texas Tallow Treats. "You're not allergic to nuts, are you?"

"Nah."

She orders a funnel cake with strawberries and a deep-fried Snickers.

The man behind the counter, wearing a baseball cap way too small for his head, says, "That'll be twenty-two dollars."

Damn, I think, *inflation out here like the stick-up man*. But I reach for my wallet anyway.

Josie beats me to paying with a tap of her phone.

"Hold up! I was gonna get that," I protest.

"No, this is the least I can do for the boy who rescued

me," she says, stepping over to the side.

"Oh, I see you got jokes," I say, and follow her. But when she turns around, her face is soft and serious.

"I'm sorry," she says, eyes staring straight into mine.

Tenderness floods my body. "It's all good."

"No, it's not. I shouldn't have come at you like that. I just didn't know how to calm myself down."

"It's okay. Really," I assure her.

But she continues, shaking her head as if trying to wake herself from a bad dream. "I was just so mad. I hated being so scared."

Replaying the scene in my head, I can't imagine the terror she must've felt. And now she's up here feeling sorry for how she treated me? "Nah, I should be the one apologizing," I say. "I'm the one who acted like an ass all night. I should've been more understanding."

She laughs. "Oh yeah. Coming to my defense and then making sure I stayed safe. A real asshole."

Her dimples are back, and I feel like I just hit the jackpot.

"For real," she says, eyes fixed on mine, "most boys wouldn't have done half of what you did. Thank you."

"You're very welcome."

"You seriously don't know how much it means to me."

I'm not used to girls being this appreciative. Not gonna lie, it feels nice. Like there's a million wiggling worms on hooks inside my chest. "Thanks for saying that," I tell her.

"You're very welcome," she teases.

Geez, she can mock me all day with dimples like that. They're straight up magic. Twenty minutes ago, I didn't want anything to do with her, and now she's got me up here grinning like an idiot.

Josie

His smile is entirely too cute. It's making me want to kiss him right here against the side of this food truck.

Shawn

"I can't with that smile of yours," she says, glancing at my mouth.

"What?"

"You know what."

"I really don't," I say, but I do. And I'm twelve all over again, contemplating whether it's too soon.

Not at all, her eyes tell mine.

Bet, my body says. But my upbringing won't let me cross that line yet. Straight up torture.

Especially when her eyes are asking, *What are you waiting for?*

Makes me want to grab her waist, pull her in close, and take her lips. Instead, I reach for her hand.

Josie

Wait, so you're telling me that I just gave this boy an open invitation to kiss me, and he didn't jump on the chance and then try to take things entirely too far?

Clearly, Shawn is not your average boy in any way, shape, or form.

I swear the way he's tracing the curves of my blisters is better than a kiss. Okay, maybe not, but his tenderness, his patience, his restraint . . . it's all swirling deep inside me, dipping low, making me want to hide my face.

Shawn

"How do you keep doing that?" she asks, interlacing her fingers with mine.

"What?"

"Surprising me in the best possible ways."

That dumb grin is back on my face, and my heart's hammering like the chute just flew open. *What in the hell is this girl doing to me?*

"Here you are. Sorry for the wait," the guy in the tiny hat says, returning to the counter with some sweet relief.

Josie

Shawn's eyes soften as he chews his first bite. Then his eyebrows rise in surprise.

"Good, isn't it?" I ask. We're sitting at a picnic table, underneath a pavilion, where music is playing from speakers on the stage.

"Maaan, ridiculous."

I stare at the pure pleasure on his face, glad I could return his kindness with this one simple thing.

"Did you get all the blisters from riding?"

"Yeah, I'm out of practice. And so is my horse, Strawberry," I say, and bring a fork loaded with juicy, powdery sweetness to my mouth.

He looks down at my plate and pulls a face.

"Ruin my funnel cake with another gross image and we're gonna fight."

"Is that right?" he says, eyes snapping up to meet mine.

I give him a hard look, trying to ignore the way his eyes are speaking to me: *this might be the beginning of something real*.

He stares back.

"Oh, it's on," I say.

"I never lose staring contests."

"Me neither," I say, already wanting to blink.

He takes another bite to let me know how unbothered he is. Chews it slow and hard—jaw flexing with each bite.

Oooh, you're playing dirty, I think, and force my gaze away from his jaw, eyes stinging . . . watering.

Some little kids run by our table laughing and screaming, and a tear rolls down his cheek.

My cheeks are dripping tears.

He finally blinks.

"Yes!" I shout, and giddily wipe my tears with my napkin.

Fighting a smile, he says, "That's why you have powdered sugar all over your face."

"So. Makes my win even sweeter," I say, and lick my bottom lip.

His eyes dip to my mouth and quickly back up.

But not before my body notices and starts to buzz.

"Anyway, tell me about Strawberry. How long have you had her?"

I grab a clean napkin. "Since I was eight. But she lives on my grandparents' ranch, so I only get to ride her when I'm out there."

"You still have some powdered sugar," he says, lightly scratching the corresponding spot on his chin.

"Did I get it?"

He nods. "And I'm guessing you named her?"

"What? Don't tell me you have something to say about her name?" I ask, shooting him a playful glare.

"No, it's cute."

Kind of feels like he's talking about me too. "Thanks," I say, blushing.

Another irresistible grin. "You're very welcome," he says.

Somebody please help me. *This boy clearly doesn't understand what he's doing to me.* "Yeah, her mom, Cassidy, loved strawberries just as much as me, especially when she was pregnant. So it seemed like the perfect name." I start yapping. "But it turns out that Strawberry is nothing like her mom. Won't even touch a freaking strawberry. I swear that girl is so hardheaded."

"Sounds like y'all are perfect for each other."

"Hey! What are you trying to say?"

"I mean, if anyone can handle her, I imagine it's you."

"And what's that supposed to mean?"

"Look, I just met you. So I don't know you. But you seem pretty strong-willed."

Can't say that he's wrong. It's just weird hearing that I'm basically hardheaded from someone besides Mom.

"You said you don't get to ride her often, right?"

"Not nearly as much as I need to."

"How far away is the ranch?"

"Only about forty-five minutes from here . . . in Hockley."

"What? I was thinking you were about to at least say a few hours. Why don't you go more often, then?"

"That's a *whole* situation."

"I'm all ears."

And eyes. I can see them traveling around my face as I speak, often landing on my lips. An invitation for mine to do the same. Staring at the slope between his neck and his shoulders, I start to tell him about how I used to spend every summer and weekend at the ranch. Busy with work, my parents needed the childcare. But that all changed when I started talking about working there after graduation.

"Why?" he asks.

"They want me to go to college and work for them instead."

"Doing what?"

"Running fancy restaurants."

"Sounds cool."

"Does it, though? Checking on shipments of oysters and truffles and champagne. So much champagne. Deciding on stemware and sconces. Learning fifty million supposedly important people's names and what they like to drink and where they like to sit?"

He chuckles. "I take it you can't see yourself doing that?"

"Not at all. I'd rather be on the ranch fishing, shooting, or riding."

"Who taught you how to ride? Your dad?"

"Um, no," I say, and laugh. "My mimi and papa taught me. My daddy couldn't ride to save his life. He grew up in Sunnyside. My mom is the one who grew up on the ranch. But now she acts like she's too good to be going out there all the time."

"You'll be able to drive yourself soon, won't you?" he asks.

"Not if she gets my grandparents to sell it."

"Sell it? Can't do that."

"Tell me about it. That ranch has been in our family for a hundred and fifty years."

"Dang!"

"Yeah . . ." I say, thinking back to opening night. I was putting the finishing touches on Mimi's makeup when Mom came into the bathroom talking about the offer she found on the kitchen counter for five million dollars.

Mimi and Papa weren't fazed by the number. Papa kept looking for his gold bolo tie in the closet while Mimi reminded Mom of how her great-great-grandparents had worked the land and bought it when they were freed. Of how hard it had been to hold on to the hundred acres and pass it down all these years.

But Mom wouldn't let up. She went on and on about how crazy it was for them to be barely making ends meet while sitting on all that money until she finally pissed Mimi off. Hard to do but even harder to undo. A shame because I'd never seen Mimi and Papa look so glamorous.

"Sounds like you need to help your Mom remember how precious it is," Shawn says, pulling me out of my head.

"Please, she's already got her mind set, and she's not the type to back down."

"That must be where you get it from."

"Whatever," I say, and smile.

Shawn reaches across the table, and I close my eyes, feeling the rough tip of his finger gentle on my nose.

Everything inside me clenches.

Shawn

"More powdered sugar," I explain, pulling my hand away.

Josie slowly opens her eyes, as if just waking up from a deep sleep. "Thanks."

I stare at her, damn near mesmerized. "You're very welcome."

"Can I ask you something?"

"Shoot."

"Are you always this"—she narrows her eyes—"nice?"

I let out a long sigh. *Not another girl into bad boys.* "Yeah, pretty much. Why?"

"You seem too good to be true, that's all."

Relief swells inside me, and I don't even try to fight the grin. "Thanks," I say, "that's just how I was raised. It's crazy, though, makes some girls think they can play me. But it's all good. Can't lose sleep over girls I've never caught feelings for."

"You've never fallen for anyone?"

"Nah, still waiting on that."

Josie

"Same," I say, eyes fixed on his.

It's wild that less than two hours ago, I was stuck in the restaurant, plotting my escape. Then trapped in a girl's worst nightmare. Only to be here now, talking to a boy who could've walked straight out of my dreams.

I swear you never know what's waiting for you around the corner.

"What?" he asks.

No way I can tell him all of that. "How did a nice guy like you get into such a dangerous sport?"

Shawn

"My dad was a bull rider, so you know how that goes," I tell her.

"Come on. You have to give me more than that."

I think about the first time I got on a bull. I was nine. It was three weeks after Mom's accident, and I still didn't want to eat or leave my room. Dad—or Sterling, as I called him then—made me get up one morning and go to the practice arena where he trained.

I was scared as hell climbing onto that bull. Too scared to feel sad or sorry for myself. And when the gate swung open, that steer bolted like a rock out of a slingshot. But I squeezed that rope just like Sterling taught me. Held on for eight long seconds. And after I fell off, he scooped me up into his arms and told me, "Great job, son! Great job!"

It was the first time I felt his love. Man, oh, man did it fill a giant hole in my heart.

In the two years he'd lived with us before Mom died, he was never that affectionate. To be fair, when he moved in, I was seven and already bad as hell. Sneaking out at night to do tricks on Lil Love. The dealers on the block got a kick out of it. Always gave me candy. He shut all that down.

Sometimes I wonder if he would've adopted me if I'd been too afraid to get on a bull. Raise a bad little boy who wasn't his blood? For what if I wasn't gonna follow in his footsteps? But I'm not about to get into all of that with Josie, so I finally say, "Honestly, I started riding because I liked the way it felt to make my dad proud."

"It's a good feeling, isn't it?

"Yeah."

"What is it about dads?" she asks as if she's thinking out loud. "It's like they have this magical power to make you want to please them. They don't even have to threaten you like moms."

I can't remember Mom ever threatening me. She was chill. Probably a little too chill. But I keep that to myself so that I don't have to tell the sob story. "Yeah, I get what you mean. Like last night, I stayed out five minutes past curfew riding with my boys and all my dad had to do was give me a look to make me feel like the worst son in the world."

"Out riding a horse?" she asks.

"Yeah, I have a horse too. His name is Lil Love."

"Lil Love." She laughs. "When's his album dropping?"

"Soon. We're still working on his last track, 'Giddy Up and Grind.'"

She cracks up again. "Boy, stop."

"What? I'm serious," I continue, loving how funny she thinks I am. "He's been going viral . . . about to open up for Travis Scott next month."

Her laughter quiets down. "How'd you come up with his name?"

"Nat Love was my hero growing up. So yeah, that's pretty much how."

"The toughest cowboy of them all."

"You already know," I say, excited. Most girls, even the ones who rodeo, have never heard of Nat Love.

"Why Nat Love as your hero, though?"

"My mom used to read me his autobiography every night before bed."

"Every night?"

"Yeah, I never got sick of it. A black man traveling around the country breaking horses and rounding up cattle and having shoot-outs. It was the best."

"I guess, but most of the shoot-outs were with Native Americans. He called them savages, you know."

"So did most people at that time," I say, defending him.

"Doesn't make it right."

"Nah, but most people go along with the popular thinking of their day."

"Perhaps, but I'd like to think I wouldn't go along with something wrong."

"Okay, maybe you would've been one of the few to stand apart from the crowd. Still doesn't take away from the fact that Nat Love was born into slavery and had the guts to go out into the Wild, Wild West at *fifteen*—that's basically our age!—and make a life for himself. And not only did he survive, he wrote a whole book about it," I say, still coming to his defense.

"Yeah, *The Life and Adventures of Nat Love*," she says. "My papa made me read it the summer I turned twelve. Said they weren't gonna teach me about black cowboys in school."

"Sad but true," I say, thinking about the book. About how Nat and other black cowboys worked side by side with white cowboys and vaqueros on cattle drives and ranches, about how they all considered each other family. Why wouldn't people want kids to know that part of American history?

"My papa says it's too empowering."

"And unifying too," I say, adding my two cents.

"It's still crazy to me that one in four cowboys was black."

"I know, right. You'd never know it from the old western movies."

"Oh, don't *even* get my papa started about old westerns," she says. "He could talk for a week straight about them leaving out the real stories of black cowboys. Didn't want to give them the credit for their role in settling the American West."

Dad has talked about similar things, but usually I'd be half listening, slumped in the passenger seat, staring out of the window at a blur of scrubby bushes, dry grass, and mountains in the distance.

"Or their actual stories!" she continues. "Change a few details here and there, put a white man in as the lead, and voilà, don't have to mention the black cowboy's name."

"Dang, that's messed up."

"Tell me about it. Like there was this one man. What's his name . . . what's his name? Britt Johnson, that's it. Anyway, these Native American raiders kidnapped his wife and kids, and he spent seven years trying to get them back. And against all odds, he did."

"Wow," I say, loving the fact that she's teaching me things.

"Great story, right? Guess who played him in the movie?"

"Clint Eastwood?"

"Close," she says. "John Wayne."

"Of course," I say, both of us cracking up.

Our laughter fades. And now we're just sitting here staring at each other, again, like it's the most natural thing in the world. We stay like that—eyes hooked, silent—until the space between us feels ready to explode.

"So you live out in the country?" she asks.

"Nah, Acres Homes?"

"Where is that?"

"Only about twenty minutes from downtown. You don't know about the Fo-Fo?"

"The Four-Four?"

"Nah, you gotta say it right. The Fo-Fo."

She has a blank look on her face.

"You know, where Paul Wall and Slim Thug grew up."

"Oh, I know Slim Thug. He comes into the restaurants sometimes."

"Well, he's from where I'm from. On the Northside."

She's still looking like she has no clue what I'm talking about. So I decide to break out a little history lesson of my own. Tell her how Acres Homes was founded around WWI and was once the largest black community in the South. At first, it was unincorporated, which meant it didn't have electricity and running water and stuff like that. But it also meant that the land was cheap and there were no rules about keeping farm animals. Of course, the city eventually came in, but people kept their horses and chickens.

"So it's like a patch of country in the city?" she asks.

"Nah, it's the hood now," I say, and laugh. "It's changing, though. Lots of development. But some people still have their family's land and ride horses around and stuff like that."

"On the streets?"

"We have some riding trails that go through wooded lots, and we ride along the bayou. But yeah, we ride on the streets too. On any given day, you might see somebody on horseback in line at a drive-through."

"No way," she says, and laughs.

"Yeah, or in the carpool line picking up their kid from school."

"Boy, you play too much," she says, and laughs even harder.

"I'm serious. You'll have to come visit me and see."

She gets shy and lowers her eyes for a second. Now they're back. "Okay."

And right on time, "Texas Hold 'Em" starts playing. "Wanna dance?" I ask her. Ain't met a girl yet who can refuse dancing to Beyoncé.

Josie

Sometimes I forget that not all black people can dance. It's like, didn't you ever clap along to the church choir? Doesn't your daddy pat his leg and bop his head to the music while he's driving? Now, you can't tell me that you didn't grow up having dance-offs with your cousins at all the family gatherings.

Things I'll have to clear up later with Shawn. Right now, I'm trying to teach him this line dance. "Heel, heel, toe, toe, heel, toe, heel, toe, turn," I say as I show him the steps in front of the stage, where people have created a dance floor.

I don't know what Shawn's feet are doing, but they're not following instructions and they're not on beat. He's trying, but he's two steps too slow and gets completely messed up after the turn. Keeps going left when everyone else is going right. And after he bumps into the big dude with the mullet a few times, I take Shawn's hand and pull him off to the side.

My body should be used to Josie holding my hand, but it's not. When she lets go, I think it's about to calm down. But then she starts dancing in front of me.

It ain't got a chance now.

Part of me wants to tell her that there's no use. That when it comes to dancing, the connection between my brain and feet is about as staticky as the radio while driving across the country. But ain't no way I'm putting this to an end.

The way she keeps flashing me smiles as she turns back to check on me and my feet. The way she's singing along and moving with such freedom and ease. And man, her body. I'm trying to be respectful but damn. She's strong and soft in all the right places. Athletic arms and legs, curvy hips, and a plump—let's not even go there.

Josie

Just when I think Shawn is starting to benefit from my private lesson, a slow song starts. Nervous, I turn around.

His eyes are waiting for mine. "May I have this dance?" he asks.

I smile and say, "Yes," loving how much of a gentleman he is. He might be the sweetest boy I've ever met. Not syrupy sweet. More like tea-cake sweet—subtle enough to eat all day long.

We place our hats on the stage behind us and step closer to each other. Now his strong hands are on my hips, and I'm buzzing as we slowly rock side to side.

He can handle the two-step just fine.

With my hands around his strong neck, I do everything in my power to contain myself. Hard when I love the way he smells—like leather and fresh soap. When I love the way his thumbs are hooked in the loops of my jean shorts. When the space he's keeping between our hips, chests, cheeks, and lips literally feels electric.

All I'd have to do is dip my head a little, and my lips would meet hers. I bet they're super soft and taste like strawberry. Man, I want to know so bad.

Josie

Every cell in my body is itching for his lips.

Shawn

"I'm so glad I met you," I whisper in her ear, doubting there's another girl as special. If there is, I sure haven't met her. Not in Texas or Tennessee or Arkansas or Louisiana or Alabama or California or any of the other states me and Dad have ever been rodeoing.

Josie

How do you tell a boy that you just met that you like him more than any boy you've ever known without sounding crazy? How do you tell him that you think he's amazing? That's what I'm trying to figure out. But I can never get my words, the ones jam-packed with feeling, to come to me fast enough.

Shawn

"I know we didn't meet under good circumstances," I say, her sweet-smelling hair tickling my face. "But this almost feels like a God thing . . . like I was there at the perfect time . . . and it led us to this."

I slide my lips across her soft cheek. *Damn, finally—*

Maybe I went too far, got too deep. Because now her eyes and hands are off me. And she's grabbing her hat and backing away without saying anything.

"What the hell do you think you're doing?" a woman shouts from behind me.

I turn around and see a couple who look like straight up rodeo royalty. Josie's parents. Her dad is tall and dressed in all black—cattleman hat, collared shirt, blazer, jeans—which makes his silver bolo tie, belt buckle, and watch stand out. Clean as hell. He's come a long way from Sunnyside.

Josie is already in his arms. "I just wanted to get on some rides," she says, voice timid as my two-year-old sister when she got caught coloring on the walls of her bedroom.

"Have you lost your mind?" her mom says. Looks like one of those glamorous women from the reality shows Shelly likes to watch. "We were worried sick. Anything could've happened to you! And where is your jacket?"

"This boy . . . he . . . he shoved me, and it got ruined," Josie says, fidgeting with her hat.

"What boy?" her dad says in a deep voice, looking ready to charge me up.

"No, not him," Josie cuts in, her voice a little stronger. "This is the boy who rescued me and made sure I stayed safe."

A warm feeling spreads inside my chest, and I smile at Josie, but not too much in front of her dad. I walk chin up toward her parents. Ready to introduce myself.

But her dad is reaching for his wallet. Pulling out a crisp hundred-dollar bill. Holding it out to me, he says, "Here you go, son, for your troubles."

I stare at the money, feeling small. *But didn't he just hear Josie? I'm a hero, not a charity case.*

I look at Josie, not knowing what I want her to do or say. Tell her parents that she likes me? *Maybe that's asking too much.* At least let them know that I'm more than hired help. *No?* What about an apologetic look? A faintly whispered, *Sorry*? Something? Anything?

Nothing, so I say, "I'm okay, sir. It was my pleasure."

"Sorry, we really have to go. Come on, Josie," her mom says, pulling her away.

"Thanks again for looking out," her dad says before turning to join them.

Watching them walk off, I wait for Josie to look back at me over her shoulder.

She doesn't.

The crowd is thinner now, and she's almost out of view.

But I keep waiting. Hoping. Maybe she's apologizing to her parents. Maybe after that, she'll turn around. Run back and give me her number.

Nope.

They hook a right and she's gone.

Sucks to be so dumb. To think someone is feeling you like you're feeling them and be so wrong.

Three Rodeos Later

Josie

The lights go out in the stadium and the audience screams. The music drops, and it's like the soundtrack of an action movie building up to an epic fight scene. On the Jumbotron, a map of the world appears. The map zooms in on our country. Then on Texas. Now on a star where our city is.

RODEO pops up on the screen in big, bold letters.

Then *HOUSTON*.

STARTS.

NOW.

Red, white, and blue fireworks shoot from the ground. Make circles and explosions in the air. Then the entertainer lineup starts flashing on the screen. Images of Shaboozey, Major Lazer, Bun B, and Lainey Wilson mixed in with photos of athletes. Hailey Kinsel, she's a beast. And Shawn wearing the same worn, black leather cowboy hat.

Chills all over my body and I whip my head toward my cousin Billie. She's already looking at me. We're in the restaurant's VIP box. Mom and Dad are back at the tent preparing for some big meet and greet. Thank God they didn't make me help.

"He's really here," I say, my throat filling with a mixture of hope and regret.

"I don't know why you sound like that. You knew he'd be

here this year," Billie says loudly over the music.

"But I wasn't ready to see him on the screen like that."

"Girl, you gotta stay ready," she says, looking at me like she's about to give me another one of her the-time-is-now speeches. She's handed me one every time I told her I was thinking about messaging him over the last three years.

Lord knows I wanted to. I must've typed, *I'm sorry. I should've spoken up*, and then erased it a million times.

At first, the words didn't seem good enough. I needed to say more. But what? That I was a big, fat chicken. That I was already in so much trouble for sneaking off and scared of making it worse by admitting I'd met my dream boy. Especially because I knew Mom would've taken one look at his muddy boots and worn leather hat and completely shut it down. But how could I tell him that?

And before long, it felt too late to explain. Then way too late. Then ridiculous.

And after he started blowing up, it was literally impossible. I couldn't look like every other girl in his DMs trying to get close to his fame.

He had a spread in *Sports Illustrated*, for crying out loud. The boy had been on Joe Rogan. Had over a million followers. And that's on his personal page alone. His stunt crew, 44 Cowboys, has been quiet for a while. He was like the youngest PBR champion in history. Won it his first year turning pro. Unheard of. And that's after getting kicked in the head by the most dangerous bull in the sport. Thank God he was wearing a helmet instead of trying to look cool in a cowboy hat. That beast could've shattered his skull.

Maybe even killed him. Still sent him into a coma for three days.

I was so worried. Prayed for him every morning and night the whole two months he took to recover. Then he blew everyone's minds and bounced back stronger than ever. Now he's expected to be crowned king of RodeoHouston.

"You have to find him," Billie says.

"I know."

"Like today."

"What would I even say? Hey, remember me?"

"Not making that face. But yeah, something like that."

"Shut up," I say. I laugh, but she's right. Now *is* the time. Shawn wasn't here last year because he was still recovering. And the year before that, my parents wouldn't let me out of their sight. This might be my only chance to see the boy who's basically made dating impossible.

How could anyone compare to my tender-hearted cowboy?

And the almost-kiss? *Oh my goodness*. I can't count the number of times I've imagined what would've happened if Mom and Dad hadn't come when they did.

Shawn's soft mouth sliding across my cheek, taking my lips. Me grabbing his between slips of tongue. His hands moving up and down my waist. Everything tingling as we lost ourselves.

Let me tell you, no one has come close.

A boy with thick blond hair in a football jersey, who looks about ten years old, asks everyone to rise for the national anthem. Billie and I stand up and put our hats over our hearts. He starts singing and, for a minute or so, I look around at all the people in the stadium—over fifty thousand—with their hats and hands over their hearts too. And suddenly I feel like I'm floating.

It's the same lifted feeling that comes over me sometimes when I'm riding Strawberry in the back pasture. The wind against my face literally feels like it's a part of me. And I feel like I'm a part of the trees. It's like everything is part of everything.

"O'er the land of the freeee . . ." The boy heads into the final stretch, hitting the high note perfectly. People whistle and cheer. Then out of the gate comes a woman on horseback, standing in the saddle in a red-white-and-blue sequined jumpsuit, carrying a huge American flag with sparks shooting from the top.

"What!" I say in awe.

"Insane!" Billie says. She has skills in the saddle, so she knows how hard it is.

The trick rider makes her way around the arena while the boy sings, stretching out the last note of *And the home of the brave* to perfectly time her exit. But the boy finishes and, just when we think she's headed out with all her sparkles and glory, she rides around again.

Shawn

"Now listen, Shawn," Dad says as we approach a huge tent just outside the stadium gates, on the outer edge of the carnival. "We've got some of your bigger sponsors showing up tonight. Wrangler, Ford, Yeti, John Deere. It's crucial that you make a good impression."

"Yes, sir," I say, staring at the thousands of white roses lining a long red carpet that travels up the stairs to a draped entrance below a neon blue sign that says *Riley Ranch*. This meet and greet was supposed to be at a barbeque cook-off tent. But I've been to plenty of those and, from what I can tell, this ain't one of them.

Dad takes a pull of his nearly finished cigarette. "I'm serious. These folks can get you even more money on your future contracts."

I nod, tired of talking about money. That's all Dad seems to be interested in these days. More prize money, sponsorship money, and appearance money. And don't let me get started on gambling money. He thinks I don't know that he's still at it, but he ain't fooling nobody, including Shelly.

Speaking of, I think, watching Melvin, the king of underground rodeo gambling, walk toward us. "What's he doing here?"

"I invited him."

"Why would you do that?" I've been peeping Dad sneak off to deal with Melvin and his minions for years, but to invite him to something like this? I don't get it.

He doesn't look up to meet my eyes. "It's not what you think," he says, flicking his cigarette to the ground. He stamps it out. "Melvin has been expanding into more legitimate business ventures. You already know he built those stables in the neighborhood, and I'm helping to facilitate his plan to—"

"It's okay, Dad," I interrupt, not trying to hear another one of his elaborate stories. Plus, Melvin's stables are a joke, nothing but a money-laundering scheme, and Dad knows it. They don't allow turnout for more than an hour a day. Can't imagine keeping Lil Love locked up like that.

"People change, Shawn. We have to stay open to all the possibilities."

Melvin's sickeningly sweet cologne reaches us before he does. "Good to see you, Sterling," he says, shaking Dad's hand. Then he reaches for mine.

When I don't extend it, Dad gives me a stern look.

I can't believe this. Growing up, Dad always told me to stay clear of this man. And now he's making me shake his hand? It's just as sweaty as he is slimy, and I wipe my palm on my jeans.

"Shall we," Dad says, and cuts me a look.

I let the two of them go ahead, Dad slightly dragging his right leg. His fractured hip never healed after Cyclone King sent him flying into the steel bucking chute. *Like a two-hundred-pound Frisbee*, the announcer said at the time.

Sometimes I wonder if it's all worth it. The scars, broken ribs, bruised kidneys, ripped muscles, knocked-out teeth—the countless permanent injuries and encounters with death. *Death.* Ain't no coming back from that. And yet, we risk it every time we climb onto the back of a bull and rope up.

I remember waking up in the hospital with tubes in my nose, so grateful to be alive that I said never again. But Dad told me that we couldn't let the bull win. Said we had to fight through pain and injury to be the ultimate victors. But looking at him now—limping and increasingly compromising his morals, marriage, and savings for another hit of adrenaline—I doubt that this is what winning looks like.

Inside the tent, the first thing I see is a huge dripped-out horse. Gotta be at least ten feet tall and wrapped in what looks like a million gold chains. *And* it's wearing a bandana. Man, I've never seen a horse so gangster.

"Hot towel, sir?" a woman in a black shirt and vest says. She's holding a silver tray of neatly rolled washcloths like the flight attendants in first class.

"Thanks," I say, and wipe my hands. Enjoying the warmth of the towel, I look around. *Damn.* Looks more like a million-dollar wedding than a cook-off tent. Dozens of white roses float above the tables like big clouds. The wooden walls are so shiny people could use them for selfies. Huge antler light fixtures hang from the draped ceiling, and stuffed deer heads poke out between paintings in thick gold frames that look like they belong in a museum. All of that on top of marble bars, studded leather chairs, and another dripped-out horse.

"Everyone's in the saloon," a different lady in the same black uniform says. Holding a tray of used towels, she waves her free hand toward a room connected to the dining area.

"Why didn't you tell me this was gonna be so fancy? I feel underdressed," I say as Dad hangs back to walk beside me. Through the wooden beams, I can see that the room is packed with men in jackets and women in glamorous rodeo outfits. I'm in my usual white tee and jeans. My hat's the only reason I even halfway fit in.

"Don't you realize that all these people are here to see you? You're the star, son. You're perfect the way you are."

It feels weird when Dad talks like this. It's almost as if he's talking about someone else. That is, until I step into the room and all eyes and phones are on me.

A lady in a wide-brimmed white hat and diamond necklace bolts from a velvet sofa and charges straight at me. Now she's holding out a photo for me to sign. Wait, I've never seen this one before. I'm on the back of Hellfire.

A sudden flashback of being on the ground. Dirt stinging my eyes. Hooves coming toward my head as I lie there, unable to stop them. Bracing myself and praying that I make it out alive. *Snap out of it, Shawn!* I think before smiling and signing the photo.

"Shawn, come over here. I got some people I want you to meet before you get too busy," Dad says, leading me toward a couple standing in the corner already talking to Melvin. "This is my son, Shawn," he says proudly.

Melvin steps out of the way and I see their faces. *You've gotta be kidding me.*

"And, Shawn, these are the fine owners of this beautiful restaurant, our hosts, Mr. and Mrs. Riley," Dad says, introducing Josie's parents.

Feelings of humiliation and unworthiness flood me all over again, and I want to get as far away from this place as I can.

But her dad is reaching for my hand. "*The* Shawn Williams," he says with a firm grip. "You've had quite the last couple of years. I must say, I'm very impressed."

"Yes," her mom interjects, extending her hand. "It's wonderful to meet you. We've absolutely loved following your journey. Your grit and determination make you the perfect role model for this generation."

"Thanks," I say, searching both of their eyes for a hint of recognition.

Nope. They don't remember regular ole Shawn. Only saw him as hired help. Oh, but that new Shawn. The shiny, famous one. They have all the love and respect in the world for him.

Josie's mom continues, "We're really looking forward to working with you. You'll be the perfect complement to our brand when we—"

"Oh, Cynthia, it's much too soon for business talk," Josie's dad cuts in. "We'll have plenty of time for that later. For now, there are lots of hors d'oeuvres circulating. And the bar is open. We have some great mocktails too. Please, enjoy yourself."

"We appreciate it," Dad says.

"Now, those are the kind of folks you want to be connected to. They're making moves," Dad says after we reach the marble bar that stretches the whole length of the lounge.

I don't know what he has planned with Josie's parents or how Melvin is involved. But as I stand here, trying to resist the urge to look around for Josie, I can tell you this: I want no part of it.

Josie

"Do you think we can take down that mirror behind the sofa and maybe put some art up there instead?" asks the photographer, blue eyes momentarily glancing up from her camera.

"No problem," I say, still a little out of breath from rushing over here. Just walked in. Don't even have time to sneak a piece of brisket from the kitchen. It's 8:45 a.m., and the talent is supposed to be here at nine.

Hopefully they're not the early kind. Mom was so frazzled this morning that she didn't even give me the run of show. A refrigerator broke down overnight at one of our restaurants in the city and all the food had to be tossed out.

"Just the nightmare I need to kick off my Monday morning," she said before banging some hangers around in my closet, throwing an acceptable outfit on my bed, and rushing out.

I walk over to the mirror. A gold, three-paneled antique with longhorns stretching over the top. I could use some help, but Dad is neck deep in deliveries.

Don't want to bother the photographer. Could ask her assistant, but when I look at him, he's suddenly busy searching for something in one of the equipment bags.

I'm not about to beg. I stretch my arms around the thick

frame. Lift the mirror off the hook. It's heavy, but I think I got it. Oh, wait. No, I don't.

"Here, let me help," a voice says.

I know who it is before I even look up.

His face less than six inches from mine, his strong arms take the weight of the mirror.

I can barely believe it. Billie and I looked for him all weekend. Tried to get backstage after the opening ceremony, but we didn't have the right passes. And after that, we searched for him all over the carnival. Came back Saturday and Sunday and did the same thing. I must've ridden the Ferris wheel ten times to see if I could spot him. I even went back to that pavilion and hung around until midnight to see if he'd show. And now here he is.

"You can let go," he says.

But I don't want to. I want to stay right here and take in his dark brown eyes—*oh, how I've missed them.* The way his lashes still curl back to touch his lids. His beautiful brown skin. The new scar above his left brow. I imagine running my finger along it, then kissing it.

"You can let go," Shawn repeats.

"Oh, thanks," I say, snapping out of it and releasing the mirror.

"Where do you want it?"

"Over here along the bar is good," I answer, still in disbelief. He's finer than he already was. Taller and definitely more built. And even though he's basically wearing the same outfit I met him in—white tee and jeans set off by his big championship buckle and cowboy boots—he looks more polished. *Where's the hat?* I wonder before I spot it on the sofa.

He sets the mirror down and runs a finger along the sweeping curve of the longhorn, all the way to the pointy tip.

I sigh. "Look at you, still coming to my rescue."

Shawn

There she goes again, looking at me that way she does, like I'm somebody special to her.

"You're about to have my eyes gouged out by a mirror before I even get my first ride," I say.

She smiles. "Can't have that, superstar." She looks older now and somehow even more beautiful. Her cheekbones more pronounced. Her eyes even more intense, which I would've thought impossible. And her hair, long and wavy before, is now cut blunt above her shoulders with bangs that give her face the perfect frame.

"Whatever. I'm the same ole Shawn I've always been. Just a regular dude from the Fo-Fo."

"Oh, I'm sorry," she says, raising her eyebrows and glancing at the photographer and her assistant adjusting the lighting . . . the makeup lady ready to powder me up . . . the rack of wardrobe options. "Didn't realize *Modern Luxury Houston* was in the business of putting regular dudes on their magazine covers."

"Yeah, that they insisted on shooting in your fancy spot," I come back.

"Correction, my parents' fancy spot. Big difference."

"Could've fooled me," I say, eyeing her jeweled denim

jacket and the diamond locket hanging from the chain around her neck.

"Anyway," she says with a playful smirk. "I need to get some art over here to replace this mirror. Want to help?"

"Depends. Will it gouge my eyes out?"

And there's that cute, high-pitched laugh of hers. "Boy, it's a painting."

"I guess I can handle that," I say, wondering how three years could feel so long and then, in an instant, like no time has passed at all.

"Beautiful, isn't it?" she asks after leading me to the far wall of the dining room.

"Yeah," I say, thinking, *It's like a dream*, as I stare at the painting of a girl and dude facing each other on a horse. Knees and hands touching. Nothing but open land and blue skies behind them.

"Looking at this painting always makes me feel uncomfortable, but almost in a good way," she says, after a minute. "I don't know . . . it's hard to explain. Like, I can't imagine being backward on a horse. And at the same time, I wonder what it feels like."

"Well, at least he's facing forward."

"But I'd need to be the one holding the reins."

"What if he could ride like a pro, though?" I ask, eyeing the dude in his Gus-style cowboy hat, his gaze steady like, *I got this*.

"I don't know. It would still feel scary."

"Probably not if you trusted him."

"I'd never be able to trust someone *that* much."

"No?"

"Yeah, no way. Not even if they had your kind of skills," she says with a laugh.

"What are you talking about? You've never seen me ride."

"I've seen plenty of 44 Cowboy reels," she says, looking a little embarrassed.

Her honesty makes me smile before I realize she knew exactly how to reach me but didn't bother. Trying to stay out of my feelings, I say, "Well, you might've seen this one move my boy Rob does where he starts off riding backward and then goes up into a handstand. Man, it's wild."

"Yes, that was crazy! I don't know how y'all trick riders do it."

"Well, I was barely even doing stunts by then. My dad didn't want me getting hurt, so Lil Love had to pull my weight."

"But you were the one training him. Oh my gosh, his little screw step was the cutest."

"Yeah, that's his signature move," I say, smiling.

"But you had moves too. You might not have been doing handstands, but your style definitely added to the group."

Feeling shy, I fight the urge to look down.

"Do your friends still perform?"

"Nah, it's funny . . . even with all the stunts me and my boys used to do, we never considered ourselves trick riders. We were just having fun, you know."

"Wait . . . seriously? They don't perform anywhere?"

"Nah, Rob works at Home Depot now. My boy Trey does welding for some of the builders in the neighborhood."

"Well, once upon a time, y'all were definitely trick riders."

"I don't know. When I hear *trick rider*, I picture a small lady in an elaborate costume."

"Well, maybe if you'd imagined something different, y'all could've been the ones riding out during the opening ceremony of the rodeo," she teases.

Her words *imagined something different* make me feel uneasy and good at the same time. And now I know exactly what she was talking about with the painting.

"But I guess you *were* kinda busy being a bull-riding superstar."

"Whatever," I say, and shake my head.

"Okay, I'll stop," she says, smiling. "How is Lil Love doing? Do you still have time to ride him?"

"Not as much as I want, but yeah, he's cool. How's Strawberry?"

"Okay," she says. "I haven't been riding her as much as I should, but I plan on staying at the ranch this summer. Want to get as much time with her as I possibly can before heading to college in the fall."

"Where are you going?"

"NYU. Just got my acceptance last week. Two of my friends from school are going too. We all applied early decision together."

"Congrats. That's New York University, right?"

"Yeah, they have a good hospitality program. So, you know." She gives me a forced smile.

"You don't want to train horses anymore?"

"Well, not for now. It's better for me to go ahead and get my education. My parents are expanding and need all the help they can get with the new restaurants they have in the pipeline. After I graduate, I can always go out to the ranch in my free time. Anyway, I looked for you all weekend," she says, hopping off the subject and turning her whole body toward mine.

I looked for you too, I think, resisting the temptation to face her. Even though I told myself I didn't want to see her at the meet and greet on Friday, I couldn't stop my eyes from scanning the crowd between handshakes and small talk. When she didn't show, I felt like a fool all over again.

"Like every inch of the carnival. On Friday night and again on—"

"I was here Friday," I say, finally giving in and turning toward her.

"Wait, at the meet and greet?" she asks, staring into my eyes.

I nod, filling up with way too many feelings way too fast. I'm not ready to get caught up by Josie again.

"Oh my gosh! Of course you were! You were the talent. Duh!" she says, breaking into the biggest smile.

Which is trying to break down all my guards . . . make me confess how much I've thought about her over the years . . . how good it feels to see her again.

Can't let it happen.

"I should probably go ahead and get this moved so I can start the shoot," I say, looking away from her and reaching for the painting.

Josie

Me
Shawn is here!

Billie
Wait what?
Where?

Me
At the rodeo
For a photo shoot at the restaurant

Billie
OMG!!!

Me
Fr
He looks so good
Even better than before

Billie
That celebrity sheen lol

Me
That's not it

Billie
Jokes!

Me
And the way he's looking at the camera
GIRL!
I'm dying over here

Billie
Y'all talk?

Me
A little

Billie
Well why r u texting me?
Go talk to him

Me
Can't
They're shooting him rn
I keep trying to make eye contact but
he won't even look in my direction

Billie
He's probably just focused

Me
Thought the same thing at first
But now I'm getting a bad feeling

Billie
Don't overthink it

Me
I'm not
I've been staring hard but getting
nothing from him
Like NOTHING
Even when the photographer switched
lenses
NADA

Billie
Just wait until he's finished and
try to talk to him again

Me
I hate this

Billie
Stop
You know how guys r
He's probably just oblivious

Update?
???

Me
His dad came and said he was late for

something else
He's gone

Billie
Noooooooooo
Did he say anything before he left?

Me
Kept it super professional
Shook my hand and thanked me

Billie
Oh dang

Me
Fr
I think he's done with me

Billie
I mean y'all were at work

Me
Speaking of . . . let me see if the photographer needs anything
Can't have the magazine giving my mom a bad report

Billie
Don't worry you'll see him again
Can't end like that

Me
I think it just did

Billie
Well don't let it

Me
You say that like it's in my control!

Billie
Ok give up then
But I don't want to hear you moan about him for another three years

Shawn

Trying to find the sweet spot for my palm—not too far right, not too far left—I move my hand along the braided handle of the rope until my pinkie edges toward Rampage's spine. *Yeah, there it is.* "Tighten it up!" I yell.

Standing on the railing, Dad gives the rope a good tug.

Rampage shifts his big body beneath me, the muscles along his sides rippling. Ready to bust out of this chute.

"We're just gonna go for a little ride, that's all," I say, trying to calm us both down. Don't need another flashback right now. I take a deep breath and look up at the crowd. Their cheers vibrate inside my helmet.

It's the first round of the Super Series. Gotta bring my A game from the jump to be in the running for the semis.

Hold up, can't be.

But it is. Josie. Clapping with her hands above her head.

How? Somebody please tell me how. From this far away, in a sea of fifty thousand faces, how could she grab me up like this? It's as if she has some kind of superpower. I barely made it out of the restaurant yesterday without completely breaking down.

Man, I tried to focus on the clicking camera, on the direction coming from the photographer. But Josie's eyes kept roping me in. I shook her loose but not before I saw the hope in her, the regret. Not before the memories of three years ago came flooding back. Us talking and laughing and dancing. Almost kissing. Her dad treating me like hired help. And me waiting for any kind of hint that I meant more to her than that.

Rampage snorts, snapping me back to reality. This bull could care less about my girl problems. He's ready to give me hell.

Focus, I tell myself, taking the tail end of the rope and laying it across my hand. I wrap it tight. Tighter. Even tighter, until my hand tingles from the pressure through my worn leather glove.

"Don't choke it now. . . . Can't get stiff!" Dad calls out, and I loosen it a little bit.

More deep breaths, forcing Josie out of my mind.

Then everyone and everything else.

Until there's only the next eight seconds of holding on.

I give the nod.

Josie

The gate flies open, and the next bull charges out, twisting and jumping, trying to buck the rider off. But it's not the same as watching Shawn. My heart's not racing. My eyes are not jumping back and forth between the Jumbotron and the arena floor. I'm not praying he makes eight seconds. The man just got tossed, and I honestly couldn't care less.

I fidget in my seat. Billie isn't here to keep me company. She's not on spring break, so she had school today.

There's really no point in me staying any longer. It's not like I can get backstage. The other day, I even tried dropping my parents' names. But clearly, they're not playing with security around here.

At least I got to see Shawn hang on for the full count. And even more important, he got to see me cheering for him while he was still in the chute. Or at least I think he did. I definitely could've imagined it. What are the actual chances of him spotting me among all these people?

I grab my purse and jacket before standing up, legs stiff from sitting so long. Then I start the trek up the bazillion stadium stairs.

The concourse is buzzing with people, walking this way and that, with big sodas and beers and popcorn and hot dogs and candy. A girl wearing a purple cowboy hat to match the tips of her curly braids walks past me with a soft pretzel, and it makes my mouth water. So I head to the concession stand, already tasting the buttery saltiness.

A skinny boy with long brown hair bumps hard into my shoulder and doesn't bother to apologize.

I turn to give the back of his head a hard look, and that's when I see Shawn. Standing in the middle of the concourse signing autographs. His hat is tilted back on his head, and he's still in his chaps and vest.

Without even thinking, I run toward him. "Shawn!" I shout.

He sees me and attempts to head in my direction, but the fans won't let him walk two feet.

I rush over and put a strong arm in between Shawn and the growing crowd. "Clear the way, please!" I call out with authority. "Coming through!" I repeat until I'm able to yank him behind a door marked Authorized Personnel Only.

Shawn

"What are you doing up here?" she asks after pulling me into a utility closet. It's hot in here and smells like Pine-Sol, but that's a small price to pay for being in such tight quarters with Josie.

"I saw you from the chute," I admit.

"Oh," she says, breaking into a huge smile. "Congrats on the ride. You were amazing."

A bead of sweat trickles down the side of my face. "Thanks," I reply, even though I know Dad won't be happy. Second on the leaderboard isn't good enough, even in round one. I'm just glad I managed to get out of there before I had to hear his mouth.

The florescent lights flicker overhead, and Josie glances up before opening the clasp on her fancy denim bag. "Looks like you could use this," she says, and hands me a thick white napkin.

"Ooh, one of the good napkins. Thanks."

She laughs, her dimples saying *hello*.

I dab my temples and tell her, "You'd think these things were gold the way my stepmom acts whenever she discovers them in a restaurant. Man, I've seen her make like three, four trips to the bathroom to fill up her purse."

She keeps laughing, getting cuter by the second.

Making my heart pound harder than it did on the back of Rampage. *Calm down, boy, calm down.* "To be fair," I add, "she needs them for my little sisters. Keeps a stash in her glove compartment."

"I didn't even know you had sisters."

"Yep, two."

"How old?"

"Kiana is four and Kaia is five."

"Oh, wow, little ones."

"Yeah, little messy ones. About to have my stepmom out here on some kind of most-wanted-napkin-thief list."

"Boy, stop," she says with a laugh. "And trust me, your stepmom isn't the only one. We're constantly restocking the women's bathroom. My dad's been wanting to get less enticing napkins for years. But my mom refuses."

"Well, thank you to you *and* your mom. Needed that good napkin. Need a shower too. I must smell awful."

She lifts one of her softly arched eyebrows. "You smell good to me."

"Well, don't get too close."

She closes the gap between us and looks up at me with a cute smirk. "Don't tell me what I can and cannot do."

Sends a jolt straight through my chest, and I don't even know how to respond. *What in the world am I going to do with you?* I think, searching her eyes.

And for a minute it feels like I can read her mind.

Hold me.

Kiss me.

Love me.

Scares me, and I glance behind her at a mop bucket in the corner beside a stack of floor signs that read Caution.

"The way you left yesterday . . . I thought you were mad at me," Josie says, her voice going soft.

"I tried to be," I admit, and shrug.

"I would've deserved it."

I'm not sure what to say.

"I know it's probably way too little, way too late," she says, holding on to my eyes. "But I'm really sorry for the way I handled things that night. You have no idea how much I regret it."

I stare back at her, wanting to completely forgive her.

"You were the kindest boy I'd ever met."

Can't even lie, feels nice to hear her say that.

"And the coolest."

I'll take that.

"And the most handsome."

Dang, now she got me blushing out here.

"You basically made it impossible for me to fall for anyone else."

"My bad," I tell her, not able to hold back my smile. Part of me wants to tell her that she made it impossible for me too. That she's still making it impossible. That all I want to do is surrender. But I'm not ready to go there, so I ask, "You had any donut intestines yet?"

She breaks out into another giant smile. "Boy, shut up," she says, and lightly shoves me in the chest.

Here I go grinning like an idiot again. "What?"

"Actually, I was on my way to get a salted pretzel, but

now you're making me want something sweet," she says with a flirtatious grin.

Man, this girl is gonna be the death of me. "Let's get out of here."

Josie

Before I open my eyes to the morning, I hug the giant teddy bear Shawn won me at the carnival last night. Slowly move my chin along its fur. Then my cheek. Up and down, thinking about being with Shawn on the Ferris wheel.

Us getting closer and closer as we moved higher and higher in the sky. The whole world fading as we reached the top. Our eyes locking.

Heat pulsing through me as I looked down at his lips.

As he looked at mine.

I can't even tell you how badly I wanted to kiss him. But sensing that he was being guarded, I waited for him to make the first move. Then, instead of leaning in, Shawn pointed to the full moon and our capsule began to head back down toward the people and bright lights.

At least my mouth got to enjoy the sweetness of a funnel cake with strawberries. Thinking about it makes my stomach growl, and I reluctantly swing my legs over the side of my bed.

Making my way down the stairs, I glide my fingertips along the glossy, dark blue banister, thinking about Shawn escorting me back to my parents' tent. I must've imagined his lips sliding over mine a hundred times as I walked backward into the tent, watching him wait for me to safely get inside.

The cold marble floor of the foyer shocks the bottoms of my feet, and I realize I forgot my slippers. No way I'm going all the way back upstairs to get them, so I head to the kitchen.

"Good morning," Daddy says when I enter. He's at the sink washing a green bell pepper.

"Morning."

"The usual?" He places the pepper on a cutting board with sundried tomato, basil, and cheese.

"Yes, please," I say, and slide a barstool away from the island to sit down. Through the window above the sink, I see Mom outside on the phone. She's sitting on a lounger by the pool, still in her silk robe, ottoman covered in paperwork.

"Sweetheart, have you thought more about joining your friends in Barcelona?" Daddy asks, chopping the pepper. "I can still get you a ticket if you've changed your mind."

I think about the pics and videos Brittney and Sage sent Sunday night: them sitting on a mosaic bench in Park Güell . . . doing a dance video with the whole city in the background . . . eating churros along La Rambla . . . in a shop full of yellow rubber duckies, holding up one with white wings and a red heart on its chest that said *Dove you*.

Their message underneath—*Miss you, Josie! Wish you were here!*—nearly brought me to tears. After searching for Shawn for a second night with no luck, I was in full-on regret mode. But boy, did joy cometh the morning he showed up for the photo shoot! "I'm good, but thanks," I finally say.

"It's spring break of your senior year. You should be

creating memories, not wasting it around here."

"I'm not wasting it."

"You're not doing anything special."

"The rodeo is special," I say.

"Okay, but it happens every year."

"I could almost say the same thing about Barcelona." We just went last summer. And three summers before that. And then two summers before that. "You know Mom can't get enough of Barcelona. We'll be back."

"But, sweetheart, it would be different with your friends."

"Yeah, but I wouldn't be able to spend this time with Strawberry," I say, even though the real reason I stayed was to look for Shawn.

"Good morning," Mom says, coming through the back door with a burgundy file folder and her coffee mug. She lays the folder on the island.

"Morning," I say.

"Why don't you come over here with me," she says, sitting at the breakfast table. Sounds so serious.

"Okaaay," I say, and grab my fresh-squeezed orange juice off the counter before scooting onto the bench across from her, careful not to bang my head on the glass chandelier again. She refuses to raise it because, according to some dumb design rule, it's at the perfect height.

Mom takes a sip of her coffee. She hasn't done her makeup yet. Rare, but I love seeing her like this. Freckles showing on her cheeks and nose. Bare skin shining. Hair still wrapped up in a scarf. Reminds me of the month after I broke up with my first boyfriend, David, and couldn't sleep.

I'd come down here in the middle of the night and find her standing in front of the fridge. We'd pour tall glasses of honey milk and talk about how boys and hot flashes are the worst.

She takes another sip of her coffee, which must be cold by now. I expect her to get up and warm it in the microwave per usual, but she doesn't. Another sip and I realize she hasn't looked at me yet.

Something's up.

She takes a deep breath and says, "Your grandparents have agreed to sell the ranch."

"What?" I say, feeling like a blast just went off in my chest.

"They've received an offer they can't refuse."

My ears are literally ringing.

"I know you're attached to it, but it's the right call."

The right call? You can't be serious! I want to scream, but the words are crawling around in the burning rubble of my throat.

Daddy pushes the short, round vase of red roses out of the way and sets down my omelet and fruit. "We made sure to include a provision that will allow Strawberry and the other horses to continue being boarded there, and the buyers have agreed. They say you can visit whenever you want," he says, and puts a hand on my shoulder.

"Yes, we've told them how much she means to you," Mom adds.

Glaring at Mom, I stand up and say, "I guess you're finally getting what you've always wanted."

"Come on, sweetheart. Don't you want to eat?" Daddy asks.

"Please sit down. We're not done talking to you yet," Mom says firmly.

I want to yank the striped tablecloth and send the eggs, juice, coffee, and roses flying in the air. See it all crash on the floor. Smile at the huge mess and scream, *I hate you!* at the top of my lungs before I storm off. But Mom cocks her head to the side like, *Now*, and I sit down.

"We know this is hard for you," Daddy says, sliding in next to me.

"Yes, but you're also old enough to understand that sometimes we have to make tough decisions," Mom adds.

I grit my teeth.

"But we want you to know that we're thinking of you. Of your future. We're developing a product line, and we've been planning to open another location of Riley Ranch for a while. A permanent one, right here in Houston. One that you can run when you graduate," Daddy says, like it's some kind of consolation prize.

"But it's hard to do that when we're spending so much money supporting the ranch," Mom adds.

"So you convinced Mimi and Papa to sell the ranch so y'all could open another restaurant and sell stuff?" I ask in disbelief.

"Look," Mom says, "your grandparents have been struggling with the ranch for a while. Even with George and the ranch hands, it's a lot of work for them. They're getting up there in age."

I take a sip of juice, hoping the sweetness will drown out all the hurt. It doesn't.

"And frankly, we're talking about a substantial amount of money here. They were willing to pay a premium for the proximity to the city. Ten million dollars is not something we can take lightly," Daddy says.

Ten million? How has the price doubled in only a few years? I want to ask but refuse to give them the satisfaction.

"It really isn't," Mom agrees. "And after a lifetime of hard work, your grandparents deserve to fully enjoy their final years."

The word *final* feels like another blast, and I pop up out of my chair again. "You're talking like they're about to die! They're only in their sixties! Did you ever think about the fact that they enjoy the ranch life? Huh? They like caring for the horses, Mom! Just like I do! Not everybody wants to sit around sipping on champagne all the time."

"Clearly, we don't just sit—" Mom starts.

But I don't care what more she has to say. I'm out of here.

Shawn

Swinging open the creaky door of my pickup, the familiar smell of livestock greets me. Not exactly fresh-baked bread but something about it always feels like home. I breathe it in, step out, and hand over my keys.

"Didn't know they valeted trucks this raggedy," Rob jokes after he gets out of the front seat. He's in his rodeo best. An embroidered leather jacket with matching boots and a hat. Ain't even cold enough for that.

I shake my head and smile.

Climbing out of the back, Trey chimes in, looking clean too. Got his edge-up with retwist done this morning. "Man, if I was you, I would've *been* had me a lifted Raptor—blacked out with forty-inch rims. Baby would be badder than all of these," he says referring to the row of souped-up trucks and SUVs parked off to the side. The valet guys always keep the best ones out front. Well, and mine.

"My old Chevy is just fine," I say, eyeing a crowd of fans behind security. A few signs read, "Ride Strong, Shawn!" "Hold Tight, Shawn!" and "You've Got This, Shawn!"

"Speaking of fine," Trey says with a grin, "Tara riding today?"

"I don't know," I say, hearing a few of the fans calling my name.

"What about her friend Cheryl?" Trey continues. "You seen her around?"

"Let's not forget about Shayna," Rob adds.

"Nope," I tell them before heading over to greet the crowd—a sea of hands and shouts and raised phones. Up close, I feel more suffocated than encouraged. But I put on a fake smile for the cameras and try to connect with something real.

There he is. A young boy maybe nine or ten. Eyes wide with the same admiration I had every time I saw Fred Whitfield or Cory Solomon growing up. He's holding a white hat out for me to sign.

I crouch down to meet his eyes. "What's your name, little man?"

"Jamal," he says, voice a little shaky.

"You ride, Jamal?" I ask, taking his hat to sign. I find a place right beside Ezekiel Mitchell.

He nods with a shy smile.

"Well, if you keep at it," I tell him, settling the hat back on his head, "maybe I'll be watching you one day."

He gives me a giant grin, and I take it in before smiling for a few selfies and signing a few pics—thankfully none of me on Hellfire.

Approaching my boys from behind, I catch Rob saying, "I'm telling you, him and Tara are done. It's all about Josie now."

"Me and Tara were never together," I say, cutting in. "How many times do I have to tell y'all that we're just friends." Not exactly true. I've given in to Tara a couple of times over the years when I was lonely. Girl comes on strong. She could never be my lady, though. Know her too well to trust her. Still, I'm not about to sit up here and put her business in the streets. Especially with the way Trey likes to run his mouth.

"Wait a minute. Let's back up," Trey says, stopping for a second and looking at me. "I thought you said you weren't dealing with Josie?"

"Changed his mind," Rob answers for me. "Keep up."

"It's nothing serious. I'm just seeing how it goes," I say.

"Wasn't she supposed to be here today?" Rob asks, knowing good and well I already told him she couldn't come. He's been putting me on blast more and more these days. I used to be able to tell him things, things I knew he would keep between me and him. But clearly that's not the case anymore.

My jaw tightens and I toss him a look. "I told you she had to go out to her grandparents' ranch," I say, hating how much I'm explaining myself.

Rob smirks. "Yeah, okay."

Trey laughs, elbowing me. "Tara's here, though."

"Yeah, because she's competing," I say, annoyed.

Trey holds up his hands in surrender mode. "Hey, hey, hey. All I know is I didn't take off work today *just* to see you ride. I love you and all but it's only the semis. This is about to be a cakewalk for you."

"Yeah, lightwork," Rob adds.

"Whatever," I say, even more annoyed. They act like it's easy to ride bulls. Like I don't work my ass off. Like the pressure and pain and risk are nothing. Of course, I never complain because in their minds I'm the luckiest dude in the world. And trust, I know I'm blessed. But money and fame don't make the bulls any easier to ride. And they for damn sure don't make them any safer.

I take a deep breath, trying to keep my cool. "Well, I don't ride for another couple of hours. Your passes will get you access to pretty much everywhere. Feel free to look for Tara or Cheryl or Shayna or whoever you like."

"Aight, bet," Trey says.

Rob daps me up. "Thanks, man. We'll holla at you in a few."

I'm still in a mood as I head to the locker room until I think about how I'd rather deal with them fools any day of the week over Dad. He's gonna be late today because he had *some business to take care of*—whatever that means. Still didn't miss telling me he expects first place in the second round.

He acts like he's the one still riding, like it's his victory or loss and not mine. But every time I close my eyes and see Hellfire's hooves coming toward my face, I know I'm the one who has to live with the moves I make.

Me.

Not him, my boys, or anybody else.

Josie

The sun is high in the Texas sky, kissing the countryside and making everything bright. The fields of bluebonnets running along the sides of the road, the grazing horses and cows, the bales of hay, the rusty windmills. Even me. It's hard to hold on to my anger out here.

At a stop sign, I put my convertible in park and lower the top to soak in the scenery.

Back in drive, and I pass the general store where Billie and I used to get homemade peach ice cream in the summertime.

The small, white church we attend when Mimi takes too long getting ready to make it to Antioch in the city.

Huge American and Texas flags hanging proudly on Ms. Jackson's fence.

The diner Papa goes to every morning for coffee with his friends.

The weathered red barn where we finally found Billie after learning Uncle Jimmy died in Afghanistan.

The Petersons' goat farm.

The Abbotts' olive grove and shop.

Until I'm at the end of the road staring up at Colton Ranch. The wrought-iron sign, arched between stone pillars, looks like it would stay here forever if it had the chance.

With a hot ball at the back of my throat, I roll down my window and quickly punch in the gate code, trying to stop another crying session from coming on. After one in the shower, one in my closet, and one in my dark car before I opened the garage door, I've had enough.

The long driveway stretches ahead, and I take it slow. Every inch of gravel crunching under my tires feeling precious.

Mimi and Papa are sitting in their rocking chairs on the wraparound porch of their sprawling, log-cabin-style house when I come around the cul-de-sac. Cutting the engine, I suddenly hear Daddy's voice in my head:

Always approach important moments with a plan.

I must've heard it a million times. So how did I manage to drive all the way here without bothering to figure out what I was going to say?

For a split second, I consider staying in the car to figure out the right words to convince Mimi and Papa not to sell, but they're already rising to greet me.

It's too late.

I walk up the porch steps, and they pull me into warm hugs that smell of jasmine and pipe smoke.

"Didn't expect to see you here today," Mimi says.

"I texted you," I say, and bend down to pet Pattie. She nuzzles my hand and gives me a soft lick.

"You know your grandmother can't keep up with that phone," Papa teases.

"Like you can talk. You don't even have one," Mimi says playfully.

"Exactly. Can't lose a house phone. Plus, I don't need everybody to be able to reach me all hours of the day and night."

"Here, sit down, sit down," Mimi tells me.

I take a seat in the rocking chair beside her, trying to think of what to say. But a strong breeze sweeps through and distracts me with how nice it feels on my face.

"You want anything to drink?" Papa asks, heading toward the front door. Once upon a time, Pattie would be right behind him; but now she lifts her gray eyebrows briefly and decides to stay put.

"No, thanks," I tell him.

"You sure? I just made a fresh batch of lemonade. Picked the lemons this morning."

"Well, okay."

He smiles before disappearing into the house.

I settle back in my chair, the wooden planks creaking beneath me, and look out at the ranch. The riding arena and stables. The pasture where several horses are grazing. Mimi's raised garden out by the old house where I picked my first strawberry. The original log cabin even farther out, where Mr. George stays. Another cabin with bunk beds even though the other ranch hands never sleep here. The old windmill. And the wooded acres, stretching as far as my eyes can see.

I will never spend weekends or summers here again. I'll never live here. Never raise my kids here. Never teach my grandkids how to ride here like Papa and Mimi taught me.

Never train horses. Never live out my dreams. Heat rushes up my throat again, and I rock myself back and forth, trying to cool it down.

"So I take it you've talked to your mom about us selling the ranch," Mimi says, and looks over at me.

I rock back and forth harder.

"It wasn't an easy decision," Mimi continues. "As much as we love the ranch and love training horses, it's getting harder for us. As you know, we had to give up breaking horses years ago. But even our regulars take more out of us now. And pouring our experience into these young trainers who just keep leaving to use it elsewhere . . . well, that's taking a toll too."

Papa comes back out with a tray holding three glasses of lemonade and a plate of tea cakes. I notice that he's favoring his left leg. His knee must be acting up again.

"Thank you," Mimi tells him before turning to me. "We're just not as young as we used to be."

"But I can help," I say, my voice cracking.

"No, sweetie. You're about to go off to New York to learn all about the restaurant business. You chose a different path," Mimi gently reminds me.

But the words still hit hard. The way they make it sound like I could've somehow made a difference.

Suddenly, I feel sick. *How did I lose sight of what I love?*

My gleaming white BMW quickly reminds me:

1. My car of choice in exchange for working at the restaurant the summer after I turned sixteen.

2. The next summer, the same agreement. Only instead of a car, it was a shopping spree while we were in Barcelona.
3. And earlier this year, it was the promise of a penthouse apartment with a rooftop garden to share with Brittney and Sage in Chelsea for a degree in hospitality studies.

At the time, I didn't think going along with my parents was a big deal. I still got to spend most weekends at the ranch. And I'd still become a horse trainer, one day, when the time was right. At least that's what I told myself.

But now I see that different choices could've created an entirely different reality. One in which Mimi and Papa wouldn't have thought about selling the ranch in a million years.

Hot tears race down my face as I imagine my life as it could have been. "I don't have to go to college. I can stay here," I choke out.

"It's okay," Mimi says, softly grabbing my hand. "You have your own life, and we support that."

"Fully," Papa chimes in. "We know it's hard letting go of the ranch. But just think, your parents are building an empire. You'll be wearing the crown next, and then your little ones after you."

"But I don't want a crown!" I shout, instantly ashamed of disrespecting Papa. I lower my voice. "I want what we have right here," I say, looking out at the ranch. To the east, Strawberry and Cassidy are now out of the stables, grazing side by side. Seeing them together like that, the connection between mother and daughter, hits me even harder. "Look at all of this . . . this . . . this," I say, trying to get the rest of my unplanned pitch out. It's going horribly, but I wipe the snot off my upper lip and continue. "This beautiful land . . . and y'all are just going to sell it? What about our ancestors? Don't they matter anymore?"

Papa sighs. "Of course they do."

Mimi squeezes my hand. "Maybe you can use our family's history as inspiration for the new restaurant. Your mom is talking like she really wants you to put your own spin on it. That would be a good way to help keep their stories alive."

I pull my hand away. "No, it wouldn't!" I shout, back in tantrum mode. I can't help myself. "I don't want a fake version of our ranch! I want the real one!"

"Oh, Josie." Mimi sighs.

Distant gravel crackling and I turn to see a metallic orange Cadillac, with cone-shaped rims that protrude far out from the wheels, coming up the long drive. "Who's that?" I ask, imagining the spokes stabbing every tire they passed on the way here.

"Oh, that's the buyer again. He wants to take some pictures of the property," Papa says.

I stand up to leave, more hot tears slipping down my face.

"Stay," Mimi says. "He won't be long. Maybe it'll be good for you to meet him. He says he has a son about your age who likes horses too."

I shake my head, unable to speak. No way in hell I'm hanging around here to play nice with the buyer.

"Okay, promise you'll come back tomorrow, then? You didn't even get a chance to say hello to Strawberry," Mimi says.

I nod, give them both quick hugs.

Putting my car in drive, I see the buyer coming the wrong way around the cul-de-sac. Instead of steering around him, I lower my foot on the gas and go straight at him.

Play a little game of chicken.

He swerves out of my way. And as he passes, stares hard at me from under a black cowboy hat with silver spikes around the brim—just as threatening as his rims.

I glare back. Hot, salty tears still streaming down my face. *At least I'm not the only loser today.*

Shawn

My phone rattles against my nightstand and snatches me out of my sleep. Rattles again and I reach and bring it to my face. Squinting, I read.

11:44

Josie

Man, I can't believe she's hitting me up this late. After bailing on me and not bothering to shoot me a text all day, she wants to call now? Nah.

But she is calling, not texting. That's something.

Still, I let it ring. Try to blow her off. Let her see how it feels.

I can't. "Hello."

"Hey, sorry to call so late. Did I wake you?" Her words are so soft I can barely hear them over the groan of my ceiling fan.

"It's all good. What's up?" I say, mouth dry as sawdust.

A long pause before she asks, "How'd your ride go?" She's trying to sound upbeat, but I can tell something's off.

"Good. I placed first."

"Amazing . . . that means you made it to the semifinals, right?" she says.

I sit up in bed and pull the beaded chain on my lamp. "Yeah."

"Congratulations."

"Thanks. . . . What's wrong?"

"I'm fine," she says, "just tired."

I don't believe her but don't want to push too hard either. "How was the ranch?"

She sniffs but doesn't say anything.

"What's up? You can talk to me, Josie."

More sniffs and heavy breathing.

"What's the matter?"

"I'm sorry. I tried to wait . . . I didn't want to . . . to call you like this. But it was getting so late," she says, her voice tangled up in tears.

My heart plunges. I hate to hear her like this. "Nah, don't be sorry. I'm glad you called. What's going on?"

"Can we talk about something else first? I've been crying all day. I just want to feel normal for a while." She exhales hard.

"So . . . where are you now?" I ask.

"At home . . . in bed."

"Same," I tell her.

After a long sigh, she says, "I need to get up, though. I'm starving."

"Yeah, I could use some ice cream right about now. What are you about to get?"

"Why didn't you kiss me last night?"

Whoa. I wasn't ready for that. I do my best to deflect. "Why didn't you kiss me?"

"I asked you first."

"Actually, if we're answering the questions chronologically, your midnight snack was first," I say, trying to buy myself some time.

She laughs a bit, coming back to life. "All right, smarty pants. Some brisket, corn ribs, and jalapeño bread."

"Dang, now you're really making me hungry. Is that leftovers from y'all's restaurant?"

"Stop trying to cheat!" she says. "You can't add questions. Now, why didn't you kiss me?"

"Okay, okay," I say, slinking back down onto my pillow and sliding my hand behind my head. "I don't know. I guess I was trying to take things slower this time."

"Humph."

"I wanted to, though." If she only knew how bad. Man, at the top of that Ferris wheel, I could almost feel my lips brushing across hers, hers tugging on mine.

"So why hold back?"

I'm about to say something about being a gentleman but it's a lie and at this point, it's lame. There's no denying the fact that we had the perfect moment. And I let it pass. But she doesn't get it . . . she's the only girl I've ever really liked, and she crushed me.

"See, you're still holding back."

I want to deny it but can't.

"You know if this is ever going to work, you're going to have to actually forgive me, right? Like really give me a second chance."

"That's what I thought I was doing?"

"Yeah, but it kind of feels like you're just waiting for me to mess up again."

She's not wrong. And my boys definitely don't help. I had to hear their mouths all night before we linked up with Tara, Cheryl, and Shayna at the carnival.

Rob: You need to stop letting Josie play you.

Trey: How many times you gon' let her leave you hanging?

Rob: Damn, dude, have some pride.

"I like you, Shawn," she says.

Her words sound sweeter than the gooey butter cake ice cream in the fridge.

"And I'm talking about a lot. So I don't want to do this if you're only going to give me little guarded pieces of yourself," she continues. "I want all of you."

"All?" I ask playfully, feeling the hope I've been keeping locked up trying to bust out of the gate.

"Yes, all."

"So I can't keep anything to myself?"

"Well, I won't be hopping onto the backs of any bulls with you. So you can keep that."

"Shoot, I don't even know if I want to keep that," I say. I can't believe I just let those words fly out of my mouth. I've barely allowed myself to even think them.

Josie

"No?" I ask. I was waiting on him to say he liked me back, but I guess I'll settle for him opening up.

"Nah, forget it. I was just talking."

Part of me wants to be like, *Come on, Shawn*. But I'm not about to beg. I promised myself I'd put it all out there this time. Hold nothing back. But now it's him. Frustrated, I roll out of bed and wiggle my feet into my pink slippers.

Sounds like he finally got out of bed too, because I hear the clink of silverware. He's being quiet, like he's waiting for me to speak. But I'm not saying anything else.

The house is dark, only the security light outside shining through the window at the end of the hall. I flip the switch to the chandelier above the staircase and head down to the kitchen.

"Okay," he finally says, his voice softening. "I don't know . . . bull riding has done a lot for me. And I'm grateful . . . I truly am. But . . . it also almost killed me. And I take that risk every time I ride. So . . . it's like, is it really worth my life?"

I get a flash of the thick scar above his left brow as I flip on the light in the kitchen. "Right . . ."

"I mean, you only get one life."

"Tell me about it," I say, thinking about the ranch and

the dream I'll never get to live.

"Plus, I don't even love it like that."

"No?"

"Nah," he says. "After my mom died, bull riding was pretty much the only way my dad knew how to connect with me. Well, at the time, he was just my mom's boyfriend, but yeah . . ."

I wish I could reach through the phone and wrap my arms around him. "I'm sorry about your mom."

"It's all good. It's been almost ten years since the accident now. My grandma was driving. She didn't make it either. It was a *lot* at the time. Doubt I would've made it through without my dad."

"I can't imagine."

A pause before Shawn says, "Anyway, enough of my sob story."

I can't believe that Shawn finally opened up to me, like allll the way up, and the only thing I had to say was *I can't imagine*. So stupid and generic.

"Did you get your brisket?" he asks.

"Yep, standing over the pan."

"Oh, it's eat-straight-out-of-the-pan good?"

"Umm," I say, searching for a way back to the conversation about his mom and grandma, his mom's boyfriend becoming his dad, and how it all relates to risking his life to ride bulls. But seems like the opening has closed.

"Oh, it's like that?" he says, seemingly confusing my *umm* for *mmm*. "Nah, I'm not having it. Y'all ain't got nobody over there who can burn like that. Not as fancy as that spot is."

“Whatever! My daddy can smoke, sauté, braise, poach, fry. You name it, he can do it. He has range, okay,” I say, feeling strangely proud.

“That’s right. I forgot your dad was from Sunnyside.”

“Look, you do not have to be from Sunnyside or the *Fo-Fo* to know how to barbeque.”

He laughs. “Okay, at least you said it right this time.”

“Whatever,” I say, smiling.

“You know what, Josie?”

“What?”

“I like you too.”

Shawn

I expect her to say something like *About time*. But she gets quiet.

I rest my spoon on the side of my bowl and lean back in the chair. "And you were right about me holding back," I admit. "I was pretty messed up after that night we met. I had only known you a few hours, but the way I felt about you . . . I don't know . . ."

"What?" she asks, her voice soft.

A massive pressure builds in my chest.

"Tell me . . . how did you feel?" she whispers.

I take a deep breath. "To be honest, I felt lucky," I confess, and reward myself with another spoonful of creamy deliciousness.

"Lucky?"

"Well, I'd never met a girl like you before. Someone who was all the things [illegible] strong and beautiful and cool and smart." I keep going. "You even knew about Nat Love. Man, what! And on top of all of that, you loved horses. Let me tell you, I was done. Like done-done."

She stays quiet.

"And then we danced. . . . Don't even get me started

about the way I felt with your hands around my neck."

"How'd you feel?" she whispers.

Last spoonful of sweet gooeyness dissolving on my tongue, I say, "Like I never wanted it to end."

Josie

Suddenly, I want to be under the covers with *I never wanted it to end* playing on repeat. I put the brisket away and carry his words with me upstairs.

"What are you doing?" Shawn asks after a while.

"Getting back in bed."

"How you gonna just leave me in the kitchen like that?"

Makes me giggle. "Sorry, I didn't realize that you were still eating your ice cream."

"Oh, that's been gone."

"Well, you better hurry up, because I'm already under my covers with the lights out."

"Word?"

"Mm-hmm, snuggled up with that bear you won me."

"You trying to make me jealous or something?"

"Maybe a little."

"Humph." He says it like he's mad, but I know he's not.

"He tried to kiss me, you know. But I told him that I'm saving myself."

"For me?"

"Who else?"

Shawn

Now she's out here making it sound like I'm the only one. Can't assume that, though. Would be a quick way to play myself. "Beats me . . . I don't know who else you're talking to."

"No one," she whispers. "Are you talking to anyone?"

"Nah," I tell her before I climb into bed and turn off my lamp.

"Do you want to talk to anyone else?"

"Nope."

"Me neither," she says.

Something I've never felt before—something warm and golden—spreads out over my chest. Thank God I answered the phone. This feels way, waaaaay better than pride.

Josie

"Do you have to ride again tomorrow?" I ask him.

"Mmm, what's tomorrow again?" He sounds dazed.

"Thursday."

"Nah, I have to train in the morning, but I'm done after that."

"You feel like going out to the ranch? I told my grandparents that I'd be back tomorrow."

"Yeah, that'd be cool."

The giant smile in his voice makes me smile too. "But I have to warn you that there's a lot going on."

"Is that what was bothering you earlier?"

"Yeah, but I'd rather talk about it tomorrow. I don't want to ruin how I feel right now."

"And how is that?" he asks softly.

"Good," I tell him. "Too good."

"No such thing."

An invitation for me to be greedy. "Okay, then . . . tell me something sweet before we get off the phone."

Shawn

"Like what?" I ask, eyes closed, right leg sticking out from underneath the covers.

"Anything," she whispers.

"I can't wait to see you tomorrow."

"See me? That's it?"

This girl. "And kiss you," I say, imagining her thick, curvy lips on mine.

Josie

"I literally just felt that," I tell him.

"Nah, you haven't felt anything yet."

Somebody help me, I think, whole body tingling.

"Goodnight, Josie."

"Goodnight."

Shawn

This is the life, I think, heading up a long gravel drive, the world 90 percent sky. Miles of flat land running along both sides of my truck and a sprawling log cabin ahead. Now I can see why Josie wanted to meet me here instead of waiting for me to finish training. Man, if my people were sitting on a piece of property like this, I'd be out here every second I could too.

Don't get me wrong, I love where I'm from. I do. But one day, I want to call a place like this home. Wide-open land and endless blue skies always do something special to me. Make me feel free and at ease. Closer to God.

Pulling around the cul-de-sac, I see Josie in the arena riding a chestnut roan with a speckled coat. Must be Strawberry. Her long mane has a reddish-brown color and she has white socks on all her legs but one.

I step out of the car, enjoying the bright sun and cool, crisp air that swept in overnight. Knocked the temperature down to the sixties. Perfect for riding.

Josie looks like a natural in the saddle. Body rising and falling in perfect sync with Strawberry. Lost in her own world, she hasn't even noticed me yet.

I stand still for a bit and watch them, imagining riding beside her on Lil Love. Man, he would love it out here. But

I'm getting way, waaaay ahead of myself. I shake my head to snap out of it.

When she spots me, her face lights up and she steers Strawberry toward the gate. Damn, the ranch looks good on her. It's the simplicity that does it. Beige sweater, faded jeans, cowboy hat, and rugged boots. No makeup or jewelry. I mean, she's pretty with all the extra stuff too, but right now, her natural beauty is showing out.

"You made it," she says, swinging her leg over Strawberry. She drops down with ease.

"I did," I say, and look around. "*Man*, this place is incredible."

Josie

I follow his eyes to the paddocks, just beyond the fence line, to the lush pastures where a few horses are grazing, and beyond it all to the open land and trees stretching to meet sky. "It really is," I say, tears already threatening me. *Back off!* I tell them. No freaking way I'm letting myself ruin this beautiful day.

"And I'm guessing this is Strawberry. Hey there," he says, slowly tipping back his hat.

Uninterested, she lowers her head to nibble on some grass along the fence.

"All good, Strawberry. Your girl here shut me down when I first met her too," he teases.

"Boy, shut up," I say, and laugh. Then I click my tongue and tug on her lead rope.

She brings her head back up.

"There you are," I say, rubbing her neck. Strawberry wiggles her nose, and I kiss her on the velvety spot above her nostrils, right where she likes it.

Tail swinging, she gently nudges my cheek as if to kiss me back.

"Y'all are cute," Shawn says.

Now that I have her happy and relaxed, I reach for Shawn's hand and gently place it on her nose. "This is

Shawn. He's one of the good ones. So be nice, okay?" I tell her.

"Hey, there," he says, and runs his hand down the white streak that extends from her forehead to her muzzle.

She nuzzles into his hand and then lifts her head to brush against his cheek, letting out an affectionate nicker.

"Wow, she did a complete one-eighty."

"Just like somebody else I know," Shawn teases.

She presses her muzzle into his face and lets out another low nicker.

"Look, Strawberry," I say. "You're my girl and everything, but let's get one thing clear: Shawn is *my* man."

"Is that right?" Shawn says, eyes locking onto mine.

Makes me want to lean over the fence and kiss him. But I can't tell if Mimi and Papa are back from fishing yet. They could be watching from the kitchen window. And after waiting all this time to get my kiss, there's no way I'm keeping it grandparent appropriate.

Shawn

We just started racing and she's already ahead, Strawberry's strong legs kicking up dust. Josie turns around in her saddle and shoots me a grin that says, *Catch me if you can.*

Watching Josie like this—so joyous and wild and free—has my heart pounding harder than the hooves beneath me.

She looks back again and yells something.

What?

She slows down and calls over her shoulder, "Don't tell me you're going to make it this easy for me."

Oh, it's on now. "All right, let's go!" I push my hat down on my head, lean forward on Strawberry's younger brother, Ollie, and gently squeeze his body between my thighs. He immediately lets me know he's game, taking off and eating up the ground underneath us.

We rip across the open field, Ollie in full stride. We catch up . . . pull ahead . . . fall behind . . . ahead . . . behind . . . again and again until the tree line gets too close, and we have to slow all the way down to a walk.

I pat Ollie on his neck. "Next time, boy, next time."

And now Josie is beside me, beaming. "You okay?" she asks, out of breath.

"Never better," I tell her, and mean it. Riding with my

girl is about as good as it gets. Only thing missing is Lil Love.

"Just so we're clear," she says, grinning, "I won."

"But you had a head start!"

"Barely!" she says, and laughs. Then she rides ahead and guides Strawberry onto a narrow trail into the woods.

I follow her, the grove wrapping us in its shade. In its air thick with pine and earth.

"I love it in here," Josie says over her shoulder. "It's like the rest of the world doesn't exist."

I nod even though she can't see me and notice a bird flying from limb to higher limb, the sun filtering through the canopy of trees above it. "Yeah, it's like being a guest in God's crib."

She flashes me a smile. "Look at you getting all deep."

I laugh. "Oh, yeah, I can take it there too."

We ride in silence for a while. Ollie occasionally pausing and pointing his ears forward as squirrels rustle in the leaves.

Then the trees thin and soon we're walking out into a sun-drenched pasture.

"This is my favorite spot on the whole ranch," Josie tells me, dismounting.

"I can see why," I say, looking around at the stretch of green surrounded by trees and a running river. At the splashes of blue, orange, and light pink wildflowers. "It's beautiful back here," I say, and hop down.

"Strawberry loves it too."

"I bet," I say.

We find a good patch of low grass and lie back. Now the whole world is a big blue sky.

"The clouds are moving so fast," she whispers, and reaches for my hand.

"They are," I say, feeling like I'm about to get caught up and carried away with them.

Josie

I slide my fingers between Shawn's, loving how small they feel in his strong hand. Loving how small I feel under this infinite sky. Loving how I feel, period.

Like anything is possible.

"What would you do if you could do anything?" I ask him.

"Like anything-anything?"

"Yeah."

"This," he says.

"What? Ride around the ranch and lie in the grass with me all day?" I laugh.

But he's serious. "Yeah, that'd be the life."

I stay quiet, mind suddenly loud with impossibility, with the pending sale, with the blades of grass poking me through my sweater.

"Now, if you're talking career-wise," he continues, "I'd definitely work with horses."

"Like doing stunts with your friends?"

"Nah, I mean, maybe a little of that. But horses in general. And kids. Like, there's this community center around the corner from my house that I used to volunteer at before I got too busy. I used to teach kids how to ride and care for horses and lead these trail rides along the bayou. Man, I loved it."

"Yeah?" I roll over onto my side to see his face.

"And I'd want to ride Lil Love a lot more too. I miss him so bad when I'm on the road," he says. "And I know he misses me too."

"I can imagine," I say, thinking about what it'll be like for Strawberry after the sale. Mom and Dad can say what they want, but there's no way that the man with the spiked rims is good with horses. I'm not having it. Just imagining Strawberry in his care is making me feel sick.

"But sometimes I wonder if I'm being greedy. I mean, so many people would kill to have the life I'm living. It's like, how many people *actually* get to live out their dreams?"

I start pulling up the grass, blade by blade, trying not to cry.

I look down. "But most people don't even try. You'll never live the life of your dreams if you don't try."

Shawn

It kills me to see Josie like this. I wrap my arms around her. "Come here. Come here."

She lays her head on my chest.

"Talk to me," I say, feeling the heat of her face through my tee.

"They're selling the ranch," she cries.

"Wait, what? Why?" I ask, wondering what will happen to Strawberry and Ollie and all the other horses she introduced me to before our ride.

"They got an offer for a lot of money . . . and I guess they're getting older and," she says, her voice breaking, "they're right. It's not like I was planning to help."

"I'm so sorry, Josie."

She takes a few deep breaths, trying to calm herself down. "I just thought the ranch would always be there, you know?"

"Is there any way to stop it?" I ask. "I mean, what if you helped now?"

"It's too late."

"But have your grandparents already signed the contract?" If I've learned one thing from all these sponsorship agreements, it's that a deal is not a deal until you sign on the dotted line.

"Not technically, I guess" she says, and sniffs. "The buyer is supposedly closing a huge deal in the next couple of weeks."

"Well, then it's not too late," I tell her. "You have to try."

"I did!" she cries. "It's useless. They've already made up their minds."

Warm tears soaking my tee, I hug her close. "Come on, there's still time."

"It doesn't matter if I have all the time in the world. There's no way I can compete with ten million dollars."

Damn, ten mil? My mind jumps to the money I have stashed in Bitcoin and stocks. I've been stacking up all my winnings and endorsement checks from my first five hundred bucks in the peewee division when I was ten. And the account has been ripping ever since.

"It's double the offer they got a few years ago," she adds.

"Just imagine what it'll be worth in the future," I say.

"Tell me about it."

Could be an excellent investment, but that money is supposed to be for my family . . . my future wife and kids. As much as I like Josie and would love to save the ranch, it would be dumb to put my whole wad on a girl that I literally had doubts about yesterday.

"My mom is finally getting what she wanted," she says bitterly.

Then why is my gut telling me I should do anything I can to help? "Your parents don't want to invest in the ranch?"

"No, apparently, they've already been supporting it

long enough. And now they want to focus totally on their restaurant business."

"So you're telling me that the restaurants are more important than this place?"

"Yeah, it's like my mom literally couldn't care less about the ranch. And my dad follows her lead since it belongs to her family."

I look up at tall pines reaching up to the bright blue sky. Then over at Strawberry and Ollie grazing near the river. This place is literally the dream. "What if I invested?" I blurt out.

"What are you talking about?" she asks, staring at me.

I gaze down into her red, puffy eyes, wishing I'd thought this through before opening my mouth.

She wipes her snotty nose with her sweater, waiting on me to respond.

"I don't know," I admit, feeling like a fool. But I'm not. Sure, I don't usually dive into things like this, but my instincts are always on point. I need to trust myself. "Maybe I could be a silent partner . . . or I could be loud and help increase visibility . . . or maybe just lease part of it. I don't have it all figured out. . . . I'm just trying to think of a way to help."

"You're really sweet, but no."

"But it's like what you said earlier: We won't know what we can do unless we try. We gotta try."

"But I can't ask you do that."

"You're not asking. This is all me."

"You just said *we*."

"I mean, if I'm putting my money in it, of course I would love for you to help the ranch succeed."

"It's too much. You can't."

"It would be an investment, not a gift. And that's only if the situation goes that far. No tellin' if the buyer will even come up with the money. Deals fall through all the time."

She sighs and puts her head back down as if considering it.

"Just think of it as an insurance policy."

"Still, it's a lot."

"But at the end of the day, if it happens, it'll be an opportunity. I wasn't lying when I said I thought this place was incredible."

"You've literally been my boyfriend all of one day, and now you're talking about helping me save my family's ranch," she says.

Her words vibrate inside my chest. "Doesn't feel like a day."

"I know, but still . . ."

"Don't worry, Josie. Trust me, I got you."

Josie

A tiny flickering light glows inside me. Steadies . . . grows. I wipe my nose again before lifting my head away from the sound of his beating heart. "You know you're crazy, right."

He brushes my tears away with his thumb . . . his face all softness. "Nah, I'm not."

It's happening.

He slides his hand to my waist and pulls me closer.

Heat and more heat.

And now his mouth is on mine.

I ease into it like I would a swimming hole on a hot summer day. His lips and tongue like second skin. Cool, smooth, and gentle.

It all feels soft and slow, convincing me everything will be okay. We glide and stroke and arch and twirl and dip and flip. I press my lips against his over and over again. We go a full five minutes without coming up for air.

Shawn

Josie is tracing the scar above my eyebrow with her pointer finger. Now with her pinkie, so tender and deliberate, likes she understands how much Hellfire still haunts me. She gives the scar a soft kiss as if she's trying to banish him.

You don't even know, I think, sliding my hand up the back of her neck and into her hair. I reach for her lips again. Take her bottom one between my lips—top, bottom, top. *Okay, let me stop.*

We plop back in the grass. And I watch the sky, feeling like I'm up there with the clouds.

"Shawn?" Josie whispers after a few minutes.

"Yeah?"

"Remember when we were dancing that first night . . ."

"Yeah."

"And you told me that you thought this was a God thing?"

"Mm-hmm."

"Well, I think it is too," she says.

A wheelbarrow of old hurt unloads. "What makes you say that?"

"It's something my papa said to me once. We were on the porch one morning waiting for my mimi to finish getting ready for church. It was super foggy. Beautiful, but neither of us said so. We didn't say anything. Just sat there in our rocking chairs, looking out at all that softness, until he turned to me and asked, 'Do you know how to recognize God?'

"I thought about what I was feeling but had no idea how to put it into words, so I asked, 'How?'

"Then he said, 'You always know God is around when you feel something bigger than yourself.'"

"Hmm, I like that," I say, thinking about the expansiveness I've been feeling all day.

"Well, anyway, that's how I feel right now. Here. With you."

I find her hand and hold it. Rub my thumb slowly over the ridges of her knuckles and the dips in between. "Me too, Josie. Me too."

Josie

Taking off our boots on the porch steps, I hear another chime.

Shawn looks down at his phone but doesn't text back. Third time.

I wonder who's blowing him up but don't ask. I can't come off jealous or insecure already. Not cute.

We step inside, and I can already taste the fried catfish, pickles, and hush puppies—*Ah, thanks, Mimi and Papa*—my favorite.

"This okay?" Shawn asks, hanging his hat on the rack next to Papa's and Mimi's jackets.

"Of course."

"Oof, I can smell y'all from a mile away," Mimi says, coming around the corner in her embroidered apron. "And who do we have here?"

"This is my friend Shawn," I say.

Shawn steps forward to shake Mimi's hand. "Nice to meet you, ma'am."

"Likewise," she says, looking impressed with the handshake. "I see somebody has raised you well."

Shawn gives her a small smile.

But I'm cheesing big. Embarrassingly big. It's weird seeing him here talking to Mimi like this. I've never brought a boy to the ranch. "Where's Papa?" I ask.

"He's on the phone. But he should be off soon."

"Oh, okay," I say, and head to the kitchen, looking forward to Papa being impressed by Shawn too.

"And where do you think you're going?" Mimi says, only half teasing.

I turn around and see Shawn still standing beside Mimi. He must've seen her giving me a look.

"Company or no company, you know you can't walk around my house smelling like that. Why don't y'all go and get washed up first. There should be some towels in there. And you can grab some of your grandpa's old clothes for Shawn out of the guest room."

Shawn

We're in a bathroom between two bedrooms. Wooden everything—floors, walls, ceiling, vanity—just like the rest of the house. It's sick. Out the window in the shower, the blue sky has darkened to orange and pinks.

"Don't worry, nobody's out there," Josie says when she catches me staring.

"You sure?" I ask playfully.

"Well, I may sneak back there."

"No need to sneak," I say before slipping my hands around her waist and kissing her again.

She kisses me back, lips and tongue hungry.

I untangle myself and step away, resisting the urge to pull her into my arms all over again. Can't be disrespecting her grandparents' house like this.

The same thing must be running through her head because she backs up and says, "I'll put some clothes on the bed."

Josie

Shawn is standing in the bathroom in nothing but a towel. His back is to me, bare and strong. The shower is running. My body doesn't know whether to slip out or stand here and gawk. It's all lust and embarrassment. Nothing else. Until I see that he's texting somebody. Now it's all suspicion and fear. I toss the clothes on the bed and get out of there.

Shawn

Me
Whatup

Dad
Where are you? I went by your house earlier. I've been texting all day.

Me
At a friends

Dad
What time will you be back?

Me
Idk

Dad
I need to talk to you. It's important.

Me
U good?

Dad
Yes, everything is fine. You've received a big offer.

Me
Oh

Dad
They're offering everything you've always dreamed of.

Me
K
Call you tomorrow

Dad
I have some business to take care of tomorrow. We need to talk tonight.

Me
Can't

Dad
I don't care how late it is. Text me when you get back.

Me
K

Josie

A knock on my open door before Shawn walks in wearing Papa's too-small T-shirt stretched across his chest and biceps.

"Sorry, he didn't have any bigger tees," I say, sitting on edge of the brass bed combing my hair.

"May fit a little young, but it's cool," he says, looking down. He runs his hand over the black-and-white picture of a little boy holding a tiny red, white, and blue American flag. The word *FREEDOM* alongside him. "Thanks."

"I guess anything is better than having my snot and tears all over you."

"Your snot and tears are welcome on me anytime." Another chime and Shawn groans before pulling his phone out of Papa's jeans—a little short but plenty of room in the waist and thighs.

"Who keeps texting you?" I ask, and put down my comb on the nightstand. Couldn't help myself.

"My dad," he says, and sits down on the bed beside me.

I look over and read:

Dad
What time do you plan on being home?

I don't know if Shawn's intentionally showing me his screen or not, but either way, I'm grateful. Most boys make it a point to hide their phones even when they're just playing stupid video games. It's like they get pleasure out of keeping girls guessing. Clearly, Shawn is not most boys.

"Man, I told him I would text him when I got home but he won't leave me alone."

"What time is your curfew?"

"Curfew? Nah, I live on my own."

"Oh, yeah, I don't know what I was thinking. You probably have a whole mansion to yourself."

"Nope, I live in the same house I grew up in."

An opening. But signs warning *this-is-too-sad* and *I-don't-know-what to-say* are flashing red, telling me not to enter. I push past them and ask, "It's not hard living there without your mom?"

"I mean, it's hard living without her, period. But nah, me and my dad actually lived there until he got remarried five years ago. I didn't want to leave but understood. Anyway, I was glad to move back last year. Living there helps me feel close to my mom, you know. A lot of her old stuff is still there . . . CDs, dishes, books, some furniture. It may sound morbid, but it's home."

I put my hand on his leg. "Not at all. I get it."

"Josieee!" Mimi calls.

"Coming," I yell back.

We stand up and Shawn's phone chimes again. "Man,

let me turn this thing off. Can't have it out here ruining my first dinner with Mimi and Papa."

The way he says their names, like they're his, makes my spirit nicker, and I nuzzle my head in his neck for a few seconds before we head to dinner.

Shawn

After Papa says grace, after Mimi douses her plate with hot sauce, after they go back and forth telling the story of buying Henry's parents from a hacienda in Mexico where they eloped and spent their honeymoon getting back over the border on horseback, after Josie gives me the last hush puppy, after her eyes catch mine a million times from across the table—*damn*—after two slices of strawberry cake with strawberry icing, after thumbing through old photo albums of distant relatives looking hard-core in chaps and skirts with holsters, through other albums of Mimi and Papa in their teens and twenties, competing, Papa bareback bronc racing and Mimi barrel racing, after I slip in a few words about how fast Mom was around the barrels, after even more pics of babies, toddlers, teens, and grandchildren, of Josie standing beside a feral hog she hunted with a shotgun—*okay, I see you, Josie!*—of their son in uniform beside a sepia photo of his great-great-grandfather, a Buffalo Soldier, after Mimi breaks out the whiskey and Papa goes off on the banjo, after Mimi and Josie get tired of dancing, after Pattie finally wakes up and greets me, after more cake, yawns, and multiple goodbye hugs, Josie walks me to my truck.

Josie

Shawn feels like a miracle. Like God made him just for me. Saw into my heart and gathered the dust and breath and flesh to shape the boy of my dreams. Leaning against his truck, looking up at his beautiful brown skin and cheeks and lips and eyes—*oh, his eyes*—and all the bright stars congregated above him, nobody can tell me different.

"What?" he asks.

"Thank you," I tell him.

"For what?"

I didn't know how much I needed this magic. This proof that, yes, dreams actually do come true. Needed you. But I do. "For being so incredible."

He briefly closes his eyes before he slides his hat off my head and says, "Josie."

"Yeah?"

"You . . . are a dream. This place . . . is a dream. Everything about this day . . . has been a dream. So nah, thank you."

A dream. Proof on proof on proof on proof. And I kiss him exactly like my body tells me to. Over and over until he gently squeezes my waist and slows me down. Then I remember I'm standing in front of Mimi and Papa's house.

"When can I see you again?" I ask.

"When do you want to see me?"

"Tomorrow."

"Well, tomorrow it is."

Shawn

Dad is parked in front of my house when I pull into my driveway around midnight.

Dang, is this deal that serious?

"Sorry to come over so late, but it's best we have this conversation in person," he says as we climb the stairs to the porch. He reeks of cigarettes and loneliness. The bags under his eyes are almost black. Shelly must be at her mom's with the girls again.

Inside, I flip on the lights, hang my hat on the hook near the door, clear the sofa of chocolate wrappers, socks, and books, and go change my clothes.

As soon as I return, he leans forward and puts his elbows on his knees. "This is an offer that can seriously change your life," he says.

Man, these people must be paying him a grip under the table. Last deal, I found out it was ten K. As if the thirty K he got off the top wasn't enough. Fifteen percent of every contract. But it's whatever. "Let me get you some food," I say, and head into the kitchen.

"No, I'm fine."

"Dad, you need to eat," I say, knowing how bad he takes care of himself when Shelly's not there.

"All right, all right."

I get my leftover chicken curry from the fridge and heat it up in the microwave. Grab him a glass of lemonade.

"Look, Shawn, I know I haven't always been supportive of you riding horses," he says, sitting down at the table. "But it's about time I changed that."

I stare at him for a second, stunned, and then get him a fork and knife.

"A man needs to admit when he's wrong, and it's been wrong of me to see your love of horses as a threat to bull riding all these years. It didn't have to be that way."

Heart swelling, I hand him the silverware and pull out a chair.

"How'd you like to start riding and training Lil Love with your friends again?"

I can't believe my ears. "Say what? You already know!"

"Of course, you'd have to take it easy at first. I still wouldn't want you doing anything to put your bull-riding career in jeopardy. I was thinking that initially maybe you could let Trey and Rob do most of the stunts while you focused on the school—"

"School?"

"Sorry, I'm getting ahead of myself. Yes, a horseback riding school . . . for youth. Or for everybody. Really, it would be up to y'all."

"Hold up, are you serious?"

"Yes, there's a ranch looking for a group of young men to spearhead its new program," he says, and takes a sip of lemonade. "When I heard about the opportunity, I immediately thought about you and your friends. It's exactly what y'all have always talked about doing. So I struck a tentative deal."

I hang my head, overwhelmed. "You don't understand, Dad. This is crazy," I say, and take a deep breath. "I was just telling my girl about how I missed working with horses and kids today. It's almost like I knew about this deal somehow. I mean, I didn't know-know. Obviously. Man, I would've called you back so fast." I laugh. Safely heading out of my feelings, I look up at him. "Anyway, let's do this. How long is the offer on the table? Should I call Rob and Trey now?"

"No, it's okay. I'll be with Melvin all day tomorrow, so just as long as—"

"Hold up. Melvin? What's he got to do with this?"

"He's the one with the ranch. Well, he's in the process of buying it now."

"Man, I should've known," I say, and stand up.

"Shawn, wait."

I take a seat on the sofa, away from him. "Nah, I don't want anything to do with that man. Count me out."

"Look, this is a life-changing opportunity," he says, pleading with his hands. "You can get paid doing what you love, Shawn. Melvin is talking about a starting salary of one hundred thousand dollars per year for running the school. I know that won't be anything but a little bonus money for you, but just think of your friends. Rob could quit his job at Home Depot. And what is Trey doing? Plumbing? Painting? Welding? Whatever it is, he wouldn't need to do it anymore."

Dad's in full-blown desperation mode. Pacing the floor

and talking a mile a minute, sweat beading on his face. The only other times I've seen him in this weird, hyper state are when he needed money to cover a bad bet. But I cut him off months ago. Not paying any more of his debts.

"On top of that," he continues, "y'all would be using the ranch as your stunt training base for free. The cost of maintaining and boarding your horses would be free."

I cock my head to the side. "Come on, Dad. Ain't nothing in life free. You're the one who taught me that. So what's the trade-off?"

"Well," he says, and pauses, breathing heavily, "Melvin would take a percentage of any profits you made from performing."

"And?"

"Well, you know Melvin is in the process of transitioning out of the illegal gambling business . . ."

I'll believe that when I see it, but . . . "Okay?"

"And . . . you've been doing great . . . excellent. Well, other than that day you placed second. We need . . . I mean he needs you to keep coming in first for now."

"What do I have to do with anything?"

He sits down beside me on the sofa. "Look, Shawn, let me just be straight with you. Can I do that, son?"

I hate when he uses *son* like that. So condescending, as if he thinks he's still talking to a scared little boy. But I'm a man now. I let out a hard sigh, as if to say, *Get on with it*.

"Look, everybody is betting on you to win it all this year. I mean everybody," he says. "Melvin has millions of dollars coming through every time you ride. To the point where he's had to significantly lower the payout odds for you and raise the odds for the other riders just to balance things out. But people *still* want to put all their money on you because you're such a sure thing. It's gotten so bad that for your ride this Saturday, he's not allowing any more bets."

"Okaaay?" I say, wondering where he's going with all of this. He can't be headed where I think he's headed.

"Now, for the championship, Melvin is expecting over fifteen million in bets to come in. And he's going to take them . . . and he's not going to lower the payout odds."

I stare at him in disgust.

"So we, I mean Melvin . . . Melvin is simply going to need you . . . to not make eight seconds the last ride."

I jump up. "Have you lost your mind?"

"I know it'd be a sacrifice, son . . . and that's why I negotiated an extra two hundred and fifty thousand for you."

"I don't care if it's two million. I'm not doing it!"

"I've already worked it out with Melvin. Son, I—"

"Stop calling me *son*!" I shout, not knowing if I'm more pissed or hurt. "I don't know when you started looking at me and seeing moneybags, but it's over. I'm done. You don't represent me anymore."

"Look, it's happening, Shawn. And at this point, you need to go along. Fire me if you want to, but you need to keep placing first all the way up to the final. And then maybe have a fall. Not too bad, of course. But bad enough to make it believable."

I fight back tears. I've known about Dad's gambling

problem for years, but never ever ever did I think I'd see the day when he'd ask me to intentionally get thrown off a bull. It's hard to believe that this is the same man who used to make me recite the definition of integrity any time I got caught sneaking snacks before dinner or a peek at my Christmas presents or out to ride with my boys: *Integrity is doing the right thing even when no one is watching.* "What's your cut?" I ask him.

"I don't have a cut."

"I know that's a lie," I say, staring him down.

He turns his head and looks out of the sliding glass doors. Nothing to see but the grill on the porch. Beyond that, it's darkness. "Okay, I'm in the red," he finally says. "A couple months ago, I took a mortgage out on the house trying to fix it, but that just got us into a deeper hole."

"Pfft, no wonder why Shelly keeps leaving."

"But she doesn't get it," he says all defensive. "She doesn't understand how business works. No risk, no reward. She fought me like hell about taking out a second loan on the house. But little does she know, I'm putting it all on you. Well, against you, but you get my point. We're about to be set for life. Oh, and let me be clear about that. Obviously, no one can know. Not your friends or whatever girl you're talking about. Absolutely no one."

Hearing *girl* sets off a series of connect-the-dots in my brain. A flash of Melvin and Josie's parents at the meet and greet . . . Josie's mom always wanting to sell the ranch . . . her grandparents agreeing to a deal but still waiting on proof of funds . . . the buyer closing a big deal in a few weeks . . . the timing of it all. I can't believe it took me so long. "Where's the ranch?"

"Oh, I have pictures," Dad says, sounding hopeful. He fumbles his phone trying to get it out of his pocket and almost drops it. "Here, here," he says, handing it over. "You can scroll through."

A view of the ranch from the long, gravel drive, and I feel sick.

A shot capturing the front of the house, where just a few hours ago, Josie and I kissed and kissed. I start panicking.

I can't believe he's gotten me mixed up in this. Tears flood my eyes as I imagine how hurt Josie will be when she finds out.

"Isn't it beautiful? Shawn, I'm telling you—"

I head to the front door and swing it open. "Get out!"

"You're kicking your own dad—"

"Get out of my house! Now!"

Josie

At a red light, a shirtless man crosses the street with a tattered washcloth on his head.

Are my doors locked? Yes, but when a car with blacked-out windows pulls up beside me blasting music so loud that it vibrates in my chest, I still press the button to make sure.

The light turns green, and I make a quick left. Drive past an abandoned shack surrounded by overgrown grass. A woman walking on the side of the street still wearing her sleeping cap. A new duplex. A rusty car on a lawn. An old sofa in a yard. A pair of horses grazing in a field. A one-story with a black gate surrounding it. Another new duplex. Two old women sitting in rocking chairs on a worn porch. A mama horse and baby horse tied to a fence.

At a stop sign, two chickens take their sweet time crossing the road, and I look to my right and see red roses saying *hi* over a white picket fence. Inviting my eyes to wander to the manicured lawn behind the fence . . . more roses—pink, white, yellow, red, and orange—circling the gleaming white house. Even more roses hiding the neighbor's peeling paint, overgrown grass, and bright green Cadillac.

Minus the livestock, the neighborhood reminds me of Sunnyside, where Dad is from. But I never drive there alone.

Two more right turns and another sofa in a yard before I pull up behind Shawn's old Chevy in the driveway of a small, one-story house on a huge corner lot. Slate gray with white trim and a wraparound honey-brown deck. Super cute.

Shawn

The doorbell rings and I hop off my sofa and do a few jumping jacks. Might sound crazy, but I gotta do what I gotta do to banish this mood. Josie doesn't need to know about Melvin's plan because it ain't happening. That ranch is sacred, and I swear on everything I love, even Mom, that I won't let it end up in that degenerate's hands.

I swing open the door to a gush of heat—Houston's weather sure knows how to flip the switch—and Josie looking even hotter in her white tee and faded jeans.

"Hey," I say.

"Hey," she says, and steps in, searching me.

Nah, none of that. I pull her into my arms, close the door, and kiss her. And it's like her lips are the perfect cure, reaching down inside me and hoovering up all of last night's hurts.

She gently places her hand on my chest. "How are you?"

I leave her question hanging and ask, "Hold up, are you trying to match me?" I'm only half kidding. I can't be one of these dudes out here coordinating outfits with their girls. Corny as hell.

She laughs. "No, trust me. I was already halfway down 290 when I realized I was wearing what's essentially your uniform. But I wasn't about to turn around. I figured you had to have something in your closet other than white tees and jeans." She tugs at my gray jogging bottoms. "Looks like you're at least halfway there."

"I pretty much only wear these around the house."

"We don't have to go anywhere."

"What are you talking about? You can't come all the way to the Fo-Fo without getting the grand tour. Actually, we should probably roll out now before we get too comfortable."

She stands on her toes and reaches for my lips, moaning as if to say, *Do we have to?*

I meet them and we kiss and kiss and my whole body is like, *Nah, we don't.* And we kiss and kiss some more until the backs of my legs are against the sofa and I want to plop down and pull her into me. I break away. "See, this is exactly what I mean. Let's get out of here."

Josie

"Wheeeee," Shawn says, holding a half-naked baby in the air. And I think I love him. Clearly, I can't. Much too soon for that. But I don't know how to stop myself from going there when he throws a football back and forth with the baby's older brother. When he goes into their house to get some ice water for their mother.

When he yells, "How them Rockets doing, Mr. Harley?" to an old man down the street watching TV on his porch.

When he switches sides to put himself between me and a tatted boy walking his rottweiler but still gives him a fist bump and says, "What up, Cam."

When he hugs Ms. Judy inside the barn at Grit and Grace Stables, compliments her red overalls, and introduces me as his girlfriend. Quickly changes the subject after she tells him to stop sending so much money.

When he says, "What's good, Lil Love," while stroking Lil Love's neck over the fence. Pulls a sugar cube out of his pocket for me to give him. Tells him about the ranch, like it's not going anywhere, and that he needs to work on his speed before their double date with me and Strawberry. Tops off the water troughs before we leave.

When he briefly shows me his room with his neatly made bed, rows of championship buckles on his dresser, a photo of little-boy him with his mom on his nightstand, and a framed scripture above his light switch.

I can do all things through Christ who strengthens me.
Philippians 4:13

When he peels an apple with a knife.

Gives me a bite.

Grills us rib eyes on the back porch.

Smiles at me through the sliding door as I thumb through his books.

Praises how I set the table with the pink floral dishes from a wood-and-glass hutch, stacked high with his mom's mismatched place settings.

Prays for the ranch as we hold hands during grace.

Plays footsie while we eat.

Splashes me with suds.

Guides me down the hall to the bathroom, where an orange can of Murray's pomade and a boar bristle brush sit on his sink, just like Daddy's.

Walks me to my car.

Stares into my eyes as I ask him, "When am I going to see you again?"

Runs to get me an extra backstage pass for Billie tomorrow.

Kisses me.

Watches me as I let the top down.

Kisses me again before I drive off, slow, waving goodbye to the neighbor, still on her sofa in the yard with the baby.

Shawn

Eight seconds and I let go of Angry Assassin. But he bucks again and—bam!—catches me midair. I hit the ground hard, wind rushing out of my lungs.

Whirling dust, thudding hooves, and ringing ears.

The bullfighter steps in—*thank God!*—and I hop up, left wrist throbbing.

"I gotcha, bud," the medic says after I'm through the gates. He guides me to a chair, where his blue eyes scan me up and down. "How are you feeling? Anything hurt?"

Still pumping with adrenaline, I raise my wrist and try to flex my fingers.

"Here, let me check it out," he says, kneeling. He gently takes my wrist and turns it this way and that.

I wince and look up at the scoreboard, waiting for my number to pop up. There it is. Ninety-one. At the top.

"How does that feel?"

Hurts like hell, but I say, "Okay," because I know it's not broken.

"Looks like you probably just sprained it real good. Let me get this thing wrapped up."

As soon as I get past the reporters and out of the tunnel, I see Dad waiting outside the locker room with Melvin. Now I see the real reason he wasn't in the chute. Never in a million years would I have imagined Dad leaving me hanging in the semis for this dude. Trevor did his best for me tonight, but he doesn't know my ride setup like Dad, and it threw me off.

Plus, those extra backstage passes were supposed to be for Shelly and the girls. *I'm going crazy without them*, he pleaded on the phone this morning. *It's the only way she'll see me. You know she won't say no to watching you ride.*

Meanwhile, it was all a scheme to get Melvin backstage. And to think I actually believed Dad was sorry. Believed that he was trying to do right.

Wrong!

And what is he wearing? Out here dressing like Melvin in a bright blue silky shirt. He eyes the bandage around my wrist as I walk up. "What's that?"

I ain't got nothing to say to him, so I reach for the door.

He grabs my shoulder. "You did good out there. First place. Exactly what we needed."

I look down at his hand still on my shoulder and then, jaw tightening, at him.

He removes his hand and looks over at Melvin, embarrassed. "All right, son, we'll talk after you get cleaned up."

Believe that if you want to, I shoot back with my eyes, and keep it moving.

Josie

Sidestepping another cow patty along the corridor, I almost run into a pair of outrageously large silver spurs attached to the back of somebody's glossy snakeskin boots.

Who does that? I think. Clearly, they're not meant for actual use. The spikes are long and ruthless as hell. Somebody could get hurt.

"I think we passed it," Billie says.

I look up and see the VIP parking area ahead. "Yeah, we definitely have." Shawn told us to meet him outside the locker room. I hope he's okay. Our seats were so close that I could see the pain on his face as he hit the ground.

We turn around and start heading back the other direction.

"Are you serious right now?" I say, staring at the same silver spikes around the brim of the same black hat I saw a few days ago.

"What?" Billie asks.

"That's the man buying the ranch!"

"Where?" Billie sounds mad. She's just as upset about the sale as I am. She planned to work at the ranch as a vet assistant while attending A&M. Uncle Jimmy might be gone, but the ranch is still her family's land too.

I take her hand and lead her across the hall. "There,"

I say, nodding in his direction, "the one dressed like some kind of cowboy pimp."

"In the blue shirt?"

"No, beside him in the purple. Wait . . . no . . . can't be . . ."

"What?"

The boy is taller . . . and bigger, but I'll never forget his face. A cart passes between us stacked with hay bales, and there he is again with his squinty eyes, pinched nose, thin lips, and crooked smile. Oh, that's definitely him.

"What?" Billie repeats.

"You know that boy . . . the one who attacked me at the carnival?"

"Wait, he's here too?"

"The one in the orange jacket," I say.

The man gives the boy some cash, but he's still standing there with his hand out.

"No freaking way!"

"What?" asks Billy.

"That must be his dad!"

"Who's his dad?

"The buyer!" I yell impatiently even though it's not Billie I'm mad at. It's like, is this real life right now? Or am I having some kind of ridiculously bad dream? Because I can't even. Out of *all* the people, it really has to be that stupid boy and his dad? "I'm sorry," I finally tell her. "Yes, the boy who attacked me is right there in the orange jacket. And that guy in the purple shirt is the buyer. I saw him the other day at the ranch. Mimi said he had a son around my age. So yeah, I'm pretty sure that that's his dad."

"You've got to be kidding me."

"I wish," I say.

After successfully getting more money, the boy heads our way.

I catch myself wanting to put my head down, but I keep my chin up and stare straight at him.

"Asshole." That's Billie for you. Stays ready to fight for the people she loves.

He stops and glances at her, confused. Then he looks over at me, eyes narrowing in recognition, before he takes a step back and gives me a self-satisfied smile showing his small, ugly teeth. "Well, well, well. Look who we have here."

My throat squeezes shut, my body turns cold, and my heart starts beating out of control. Suddenly I feel like I'm right back where I was three years ago. But I refuse to let him see that. Right now, I am *not* trapped, and I am *not* helpless. I throw my shoulders back and give him a hard stare.

Billie steps forward. "I suggest you keep it moving."

He laughs under his breath, still looking at me. "All good. I'm sure I'll catch you by yourself again."

Shawn

"You still have that on?" Dad asks in a low voice as soon as I step out of the locker room. He's alone.

"I sprained my wrist," I say, looking around for Josie.

"It's not a good look. You need to take it off."

And there she is with a big smile and wave. Looking pretty as ever in her white lace top. Fanciness back in full effect.

I wave hello, cheesing—I can't help myself—and hold up my pointer finger as if to say, *One sec*.

"Who's that? Your girlfriend?" Dad asks after turning around to look at her. "You should bring her over here so I can meet her."

I shake my head. Ain't no way I'm letting him anywhere near Josie.

"But seriously, it's not a good time for you to be seen with your wrist wrapped up like that," he says.

"What are you talking about? The championship is over a week away."

"Still, you can't have people thinking that there's a problem."

"So what do you want me to do? Take off the wrap and let my wrist swell up? It won't heal like it needs to."

"I'm sure you're strong enough to suck it up."

Hurt flares in my chest, and I stare at him. I don't know who this man is. Not my dad. I'll tell you that.

He leans in close and lowers his voice even more. "Look at it this way—if your wrist is still hurt for the championship ride, you might just lose. Then there won't be anything to feel guilty about. A little pain on the front end is worth that, isn't it?"

Man, I don't even know why I'm still standing here. I'm about to bounce when Melvin strolls up. He looks down at my wrist . . . up at me . . . and then back at my wrist, like he's threatening me.

"Dude, you can't be serious," I say under my breath. But I know from all the black eyes, bullet wounds, and broken limbs over the years just how serious Melvin can get. I need to get Josie out of here.

"You know him?" she asks after I make it across the hall.

I almost tell her everything, right there, in front of her cousin. But I want to keep her out of it.

Melvin can threaten me and my dad however he wants, but ain't no way I'm throwing the championship ride. And if he can't get the cash, he won't be able to buy the ranch. Simple as that. I tilt my hat back on my head and whisper, "I'll tell you about it later," before giving her a quick kiss.

"Okay," she says. "Congrats on the ride."

"Thanks," I reply, turn to her cousin, and hold out my half-bandaged hand. "Hey, Billie. I'm Shawn."

"Oh my gosh. Are you okay?" Josie asks.

"I sprained my wrist, but it's fine," I say, still holding my hand out for Billie.

She doesn't shake it. "I think you should answer Josie's question."

Oh, I see Billie is one of those I-don't-play type of girls. Too bad my boys aren't here to distract her. They're at the drive-in with Cheryl and Shayna.

"I don't *know* him," I say. "He's an underground bookie on the rodeo circuit. Not somebody I like to be around. So can we get out of here?"

"But you were talking to that other man that he's with for a while. The man in blue. Who's that?" Billie presses.

I let out a hard sigh. "My dad."

"Your dad? And you weren't gonna introduce Josie?"

Josie

Billie is right. I invite Shawn to my family's ranch, he does all this yapping about saving it, then he has dinner with my grandparents. But his dad is standing twenty feet from me and he's not going to even introduce me? What? Am I not special enough? Or is he just full of crap?

I fold my arms and stare at Shawn, who is standing there losing points by the second.

He briefly lowers his head before he looks up at me and says, "My dad is a gambling addict."

The pain in his eyes shoots straight through me. Okay, enough of Billie's interrogation. "Sorry, my cousin can be a little extra sometimes," I say, and reach for his good hand. I widen my eyes at her as if to say, *Quit it.*

"It's all good," Shawn says, and turns to Billie. "I know you were just trying to look out."

"Yeah," Billie says. "My bad."

"Seriously, don't even worry about it," Shawn says, glancing back at his dad. "Y'all wanna get out here? Maybe ride the Ferris wheel?"

The hurt I catch on his face has me wishing we were alone so that we could really talk. But that's not happening tonight. Sage texted me a code red earlier. She's at the restaurant with Brittney and her mom. I love Ms. Trinity, I do. She's one of the "cool moms" according to everybody at school. But Brittney hates how her mom dresses like she's half her age and has no shame flirting with all the single dads. Half the time, I'm embarrassed for her. Anyway, tonight her mom is apparently already on her fifth glass of champagne and has turned the area in front of the caviar bar into a dance floor. "Actually, Sage and Brittney are waiting for us at the restaurant."

"So you want to head over there?"

I love that Shawn is game for meeting more of my friends after Billie just grilled him, and I would love for them to meet him. But I know Brittney will be in a bad mood and I can already hear Ms. Trinity's million questions about what famous people he could hook her up with.

I squeeze his hand. "Seems like you've already been through enough tonight."

"You sure? I can hang if you want me to."

"Yeah, I'm sure," I tell him.

His face softens, eyes saying, *Thank you*. "Okay, well, at least let me walk y'all over there."

Every single one of his points is back, and I kiss him for way less time than I want to.

Doesn't stop Billie from saying, "Y'all do realize I'm still standing here, right?"

"That's Josie. She can't keep her hands off me," Shawn teases.

I roll my eyes, cheesing.

We walk together from the arena over to the restaurant, Shawn and Billie debating about ice cream most of the way.

Shawn argues that Jeni's is the best—hands down—but Billie says it's un-Texan to buy anything but Blue Bell.

As they move on to Trill Burgers versus Whataburger, I spot an orange jacket in the distance. The boy who attacked me is in line at Lone Star Corn Dogs with three other guys.

"Man, the OG Burger goes hard, and Bun B is out here doing his thing. But I gotta admit, Whataburger is about as Texan as Texan can get," Shawn says.

"Actually, no, Buc-ee's is."

"You ain't never lied," Shawn says, face lit up. "Nothing beats Buc-ee's!"

"Oh my gosh, their habanero jerky!"

"Goes so hard! And their homemade fudge . . . man, what?"

"So good!"

I think about interrupting to point out the boy and tell Shawn that we saw him backstage earlier. But it's not worth ruining either of their moods. I'll tell him about it later.

"I must admit, you're all right, Shawn. I *guess* I approve of you dating my cousin," Billie says as we approach the steps to my parents' tent.

"Guess? And here I was thinking we were a part of the same Buc-ee's tribe."

"We are . . . we are. Anyway, it was nice meeting you," she says with a smile.

"For real, the pleasure was all mine," Shawn says, and shakes her hand.

An impressed look before she says, "All right, Josie, I'll see you inside," and heads up the stairs.

"See you," I say, and watch her disappear behind the blue velvet curtain.

I hop up onto the bottom step and turn around. "It's kind of cool being taller than you."

He gently pulls me back down and into his arms.

"Now who can't keep their hands off who?" I ask playfully.

We stand there for a few seconds, just staring at each other, heat pulsing between us. *I think I'm falling for you*, I almost tell him.

"Josie . . . Josie . . . Josie," he says.

"When am I going to see you again?"

"When do you want to see me?"

"Tomorrow." *And the day after that and the day after that and the day after that.*

"Well, tomorrow it is, then."

Shawn

I knew Josie's family was paid, but *damn*. Outside the iron gate, I stare at her massive stone crib with its striped dark-blue awnings, glad that I at least got my truck washed today. Even paid for the tire shine. But it's still gonna look out of place behind Josie's drop-top Beemer, out front like the house's perfect accessory.

I punch in the code she gave me.

Beep, and the gate slowly starts to swing open.

I'm in. Pull around the paved, circular drive with a big fountain in the center. Six tall magnolia trees stand outside the house like guards. The whole setup reminds me of some of the fancy hotels my sponsors have put me up in. But never in my life have I been to a house like this. Truth be told, I've never even been to a neighborhood like this.

Josie comes outside and waits for me in front of the huge iron doors. She's in a tank top and running shorts. Man, she looks good.

"You made it," she says with a giant smile after I step out of my truck. Her hair is back in a short ponytail and she's not wearing any makeup.

"I did."

Her sweet lips on mine before she takes my hand and leads me inside.

"Maaan," I say, feeling like I just got submerged in some kind of underwater palace. Everything is a deep blue—the walls, the curved banister, the carpet running down both sets of stairs. There's a huge turquoise chandelier hanging from a round stained-glass window in the ceiling. Blue and white with floral shapes. Looks like it came straight out of an old church in a foreign country. Never been to one so don't ask me where. Italy maybe?

"I know. It's a lot," Josie says.

I catch my mouth wide open and close it. Still, I can't help but look around. I thought the restaurant was fancy, but this is next level. Even smells like an ocean breeze in here. "This house is crazy."

"Yeah, a bit over the top, but that's my mom," Josie says, leading me through an arched, deep-blue hallway underneath the stairs.

"Hold up, your mom did this?"

"Yeah, she's the one who does all the restaurants too."

I look around at the kitchen—green and cream diamond patterned floors, green and pink striped cushions, glossy green tile, tall plants in huge pots that barely look real. "It's sooo . . ."

"Green?" Josie says, and laughs.

"No, I was trying to think of the word *lush*."

"We do have a lot of plants."

"Yeah, but I think *bold* is a better word. This whole house is bold as hell."

"You want something to drink? Water? Orange juice? Strawberry lemonade?"

"I'll take some lemonade, thanks," I say, staring out of the huge window above the kitchen sink at a long rectangular pool surrounded by a perfectly manicured lawn and exotic-looking trees. Six lounge chairs with plush striped cushions along one side of the pool. A rectangular dining table underneath a gazebo along the other. This house is like night and day from the ranch. "It's hard to imagine that all of this was designed by someone who grew up in the country with horses."

"Tell me about it," Josie says, offering me a glass of lemonade.

I take it with my left hand and slide my thumb along its raised diamond pattern.

She lifts her glass. "Cheers."

"Cheers," I reply, and tap with her, smiling as I think about my little sisters. They do the same thing every morning with their milk.

"But yeah, Mimi says my mom was always different. Been into fashion and design since she was like two. Didn't want to be caught dead on a horse after middle school. As soon as she got her license, drove all the way to the city after school every day to work at some luxury furniture store. And after she went off to New York for college and met my dad, she didn't want any part of the ranch."

"I thought you said your dad was from Sunnyside."

"Yeah, but he was in New York for culinary school. They met at a gallery opening where he was working for the catering company and she was interning for some artist."

"What? That's wild!"

"I guess," Josie says, as if it happens every day, like it's regular.

Makes me feel like I gotta break it down. "So you're telling me that both of your parents are from H-Town—your dad from the hood, your mom from the country. And they make it all the way to New York City on their separate grinds. And then they end up"—I pause, holding up a finger—"one: meeting." I raise a second finger. "Two: falling in love." I lift the last one. "And three: building a crazy successful business together in the city that made them."

"What are you saying? That I should forget about the ranch and be happy to work for my parents?"

"What? No, not at all! I'm just saying that's the American dream right there . . . and a happily ever after . . . all rolled up in one." I never thought these words would be coming out of my mouth, but, "Josie, you may not see it, but your parents are dope. For real, can I be like your parents when I grow up?" I say, and laugh.

Josie

A quick glance at the breakfast table behind Shawn and my mind flashes back to the other morning. . . . Mom telling me they're selling the ranch whether I like it not . . . Dad offering up the new restaurant as if it would magically make everything better. And I want to go off. Tell Shawn that he doesn't know what he's talking about.

Instead, I say, "Enough about my parents. You ready to get beat at pool?"

He laughs. "I mean, you can come catch this L if you want to."

We take our lemonades upstairs and head to the game room, talking noise the whole way. "Where the champion will lay her head tonight," I say as we pass my open bedroom door.

He peeks his head in as if it's off-limits. "I'm sorry, Your Highness, but there can only be one champion. And that's me."

I roll my eyes. "Your Highness?"

"Oh, my bad. Is it *Your Royal Highness*?" he says, laughing.

"It's not funny. I'm not a princess."

"Could've fooled me," he says, looking around.

I look with him—at my canopy bed with lilac sheers,

matching chandelier, the fresh roses on my nightstand, the antique gold mirror above my vanity, which is cluttered with designer makeup and perfume, clothes still with their tags tossed across my purple tufted sofa—as if for the first time. "Whatever," I say, and shut the door.

When we make it to the game room at the end of the hall, Shawn asks, "Does that thing work?" looking at the jukebox in the corner.

"Yeah, but it only has old CDs. Stuff from the nineties and early two thousands." A treasure trove to me, but my friends always prefer to listen to Spotify.

He makes a mad dash across the room, slowing briefly to place his lemonade on a coaster on the card table. "Let me see if y'all have the Fugees."

"Yeah, *The Score* is in there."

"One of the best albums of all time!" he says, already turning the knob on the jukebox to flip through the CD pages, sun beaming through the window behind him.

"It's amazing. But is it better than the *The Miseducation of Lauryn Hill*? I don't think so," I say, grabbing two pool balls and rolling them onto the table.

"That's a sick album, no doubt. But *The Score* still comes out on top. One hundred percent."

"Maybe to you," I say playfully.

He looks at me over his shoulder and gives me a smile. "Yes, to *me* . . . in *my* opinion . . . *I* feel as though . . . *The Score* is the best."

Can't do anything but shake my head.

"Honestly, I probably just love it because my mom

loved it. She used to play it nonstop."

"Sounds like a good reason to me," I tell him. And when he stays quiet for too long, I add, "I'm just glad you're not trying to play what everybody at school listens to. I swear it's like the same ten songs on repeat."

"What do you mean? You don't like getting your daily dose of dudes calling girls *bitches* and *hos*?" he asks, flashing me a faux-serious face.

"Oh, yeah," I say. "Gives me the same warm and fuzzy feeling you must get every time you hear girls brag about playing guys for money and being freaks."

He laughs. "Man, makes me want to wife up somebody so bad."

A serious question pops into my head. But I don't want to scare him off, so I focus on putting the balls in their proper places in the triangle. Eight ball in the center. But the question is still begging to get out. "Do you want to get married and have kids one day?"

"Definitely. I've always pictured myself with a big family."

I eye him at the jukebox—bandaged hand resting up on the silver crest . . . strong shoulders under his white tee, looking down at the music—and I'm searching for the weirdness that usually accompanies asking boys about the future. But I don't see it, so I ask, "Like, how many kids?"

"I'm not about to be out here driving a minivan, so I'd say three."

I position the triangle on the small dot at the foot of the table. "Three? That's not a big family."

He turns to look at me over his shoulder again. "You

would want more than that?"

"Yeah, I want five. But if God gives me six, I think I'll be able to deal with it."

"Damn, girl! I guess I could try to find a cool minivan. Black it out . . . maybe get some rims."

I allow myself to cheese ridiculously big behind his back.

But then he turns around and starts coming my way, jukebox playing:

It's funny how money change a situation.
Miscommunication leads to complication.

"Aw, how sweet. You chose my album," I say.

His hand low on my back. "Well, it is your house."

I gently lift the rack away from the neatly arranged balls and turn around. "Does that mean I get break shot?"

He slides his hands around my waist, same way he did the first time we danced. "You can get anything you want."

"Five kids?" I ask playfully.

"Five . . . six . . . it's whatever."

"Still feeling lucky?"

"As ever," he says, leaning in.

His lips are so warm . . . so soft . . . and I quickly lose my tongue to his.

He lets out a sound and it buzzes inside my mouth.

Whole body humming, I press into him.

He slips his thumb under the bottom edge of my tank and rubs my bare waist.

Stop, Josie, stop, something inside me says, but I don't. I press harder—

He pulls away and lets out a deep breath. "What in the world am I going to do with you, Josie Riley?"

Anything you want, I think, staring into his eyes. *I'm yours.* But I say, "How about you start by getting this beat-down."

Shawn

I should've known as soon as she met me on the porch in her low-cut tank and itty-bitty shorts that it was a setup.

"Right side pocket," she says, twisting the chalk cube over the tip of her pool stick.

"No way," I say, hopelessly trying to throw her off her game.

She bends over the table and lines up with the shot. Locks her eyes on the cue ball. Slowly draws her stick back and forth a few times before she strikes. Pops up and leans back to watch the eight ball roll . . . roll . . . and drop. Turns to me with a playful smirk. "Now are you finally going to admit that I'm the champion?"

I swear I hate losing. And to take that L not once . . . not twice . . . but three times in a row? I'm not gonna lie, I'm low-key hurt. "All I gotta say is that you knew exactly what you were doing with that outfit."

"Don't be a sore loser," she says, walking toward me with a giant smile.

I'm sitting on a leather barstool in front of a huge painting of people dancing in an old-school club. "But for real though, how was I supposed to focus with you looking like this," I say, sliding my hands around the curve of her hips. *Damn.* "Next time you're wearing sweats."

"And I'll still beat you. Only it'll be sadder because you won't have any excuses."

"Dang, that's hardcore."

She raises her eyebrows. "Look, don't come for me and I won't come for you," she says, fighting a smile. "Now, say I'm the best."

I swear I love you, I think, staring into her fiery eyes. *Like . . . I mean like . . . not love, right?*

"Say it."

"You're the best, Josie," I say, and kiss her to get rid of my confusion.

"You're dangerous, you know that?" she tells me after she pulls away.

"Nah, that's all you," I say.

"We need a time-out. Food before the movie?"

"Yeah, food would be good."

Josie

We're eating our porterhouse and okra and crawfish potato-and-cheese (leftovers from Riley Steakhouse) in the gazebo. The sky is a watercolor of blues, pinks, and purples. Light rain is falling, making a thousand tiny circles in the pool.

Bliss.

Until I ask, "You know that boy who attacked me at the carnival?"

Shawn sets down his glass of lemonade and looks over at me. "Yeah, Donny. Why?"

"I saw him outside the locker room last night."

Dark thunderclouds gather on his face. "Why didn't you tell me?"

His harsh tone cuts me, and I look out at the pool, trying not to feel hurt. I wanted to wait for the right time to bring it up because of his dad's gambling problem, but I don't know how to say that.

"I'm sorry. That came out wrong," he says, taking my hand. He brings it to his lips and kisses my fingers. "I just hate that you ran into him when I wasn't there."

A flashback of Donny all up in my face, threatening me. But I don't want to tell Shawn, so I stab a piece of crawfish.

"Did something else happen with Donny?" he asks.

"I'm pretty sure that his dad is the one buying the ranch. Was that his dad in the spikey hat?"

"Yeah, but nobody's buying the ranch," Shawn says, as if that's that. Face dark again.

Makes me not want to ask about anything else. Even though I'm really curious. His dad and that guy were practically twinning. It's not like I know a whole lot about the world of gambling. But bookies and addicts don't seem like they would make for good friends. Not when the bookie might have to chop off a finger or break a leg to get his money. But maybe I've watched too many movies.

"What time are your parents supposed to be home?" Shawn asks, unwrapping his hand like a boxer after a fight.

My stomach doesn't like how it feels to change the subject with so much unsaid. I stop eating. Put my fork down. "Don't you need to keep that on?"

"Nah, it needs to move so it doesn't get stiff and weak."

"But it's only been a day."

"I'm good," he says coolly. "What time, though?"

His wrist is still swollen and bruised.

"Around two or three."

"In the morning?"

"Yeah, weekends during rodeo season get crazy."

A long pause. Him seemingly lost in thought. Face still mad.

Me wondering about his dad.

"Aren't you back at school tomorrow?" he finally asks.

"Ugh, don't remind me."

"I should probably go."

No! I think. I don't want him to leave with things off between us. "Do you want to go?"

He looks at me. "Nah."

"Well, it's only seven. I usually don't go to sleep until midnight," I say, getting up to sit in his lap.

"You mean you don't do a five-hour skin care routine before bed?" he teases.

"I am *not* that girl."

"It's still kind of crazy that you're my girl."

"Well, I am," I say.

He wraps his arms around my waist. "I just want to protect you."

"Yeah?" I whisper, imagining him punching Donny in the face again.

"More than anything," he says.

"Yeah?"

His voice softens. "I got you, Josie."

Every cell in my body shouts, *We believe him!* And I lower my mouth to his and kiss him again and again. A pause to look into his eyes, to make sure everything between us is as good as it feels—yes!—and I dive back in.

After a few minutes of swirling warmth, Shawn wraps his good arm around me and stands us both up.

"Whoa," I say, his strength surprising me. I don't know why. I should be used to it by now.

"I thought we were supposed to be watching a movie."

Shawn

"I've never done it before," Josie says, straddling me. We're in a love seat in her home theater. Credits rolling behind her on the big screen.

The bottom of her tank top is scrunched up above her belly button and I pull it down, wrist throbbing. "I'm not trying to take it there," I assure her.

"I guess I'm telling you because things keep getting heated between us . . . and I'm not used to this kind of heat. And it's making me want things. Things I've promised myself I'd save for later."

I stare up at her, feeling bad. Her hair is wild. Somewhere along the way, she lost her ponytail holder. "I'm sorry—"

"No, I mean, look at me," she says, and glances down at her thighs across my lap. "It's not your fault or anything. I guess I'm just saying all of this because I need help."

"I got you. I'm cool with taking it slow. It's getting late anyway. I should probably go."

She leans forward, pressing her hands hard into my chest, as if to keep me from getting up. "No," she says playfully, "it's only ten. We still have at least four hours. We can watch another movie."

"Four hours? You're wildin' now."

"Well, it *is* my last day of spring break," she says, defending herself. "And I didn't go anywhere or do anything big."

"The Fo-Fo is nowhere big?" I tease.

She sits up and laughs. "You know what I mean. I could've gone to Barcelona and gotten into God knows how much trouble with Brittney and Sage."

"Is that right?" I say, and playfully grab her thighs.

"Not trouble-trouble. But they definitely did things they weren't supposed to do. Like they went to this concert and met these guys who told them about this party where they met these other guys . . . you know, stuff like that."

"Sounds boring, if you ask me," I say, still teasing.

"No, the point is—I didn't want to go. I wanted to stay here and find you."

"Hold up." I look at her in disbelief. "You mean to tell me that you didn't go to Barcelona with your friends so that you could look for me at the rodeo?"

"Yeah," she says, her voice going soft. "I felt like it might be my last chance."

"Man, I had no idea."

"Well, now you do."

"I don't even know what to say. *Thanks* doesn't feel like enough. We wouldn't even be together if you had gone."

"Don't say that."

"What? It's true."

"But I don't want to think about not being with you."

"Me neither." I stare at her, still stunned by what she gave up for me with no guarantee.

"What?"

I think I love you, I want to tell her. But she deserves certainty. "You legit took one for the team."

"No worries. It was totally worth it." She leans down to kiss my right cheek . . . my left cheek . . . my nose . . . my brow. She brushes her lips across my long Hellfire scar. Gently lifts my arm up to kiss my wrist.

I slide my eyes closed and plunge into her tenderness, the rest of the world a million miles away. *Josie . . . Josie . . . Josie. You just might be my once-in-a-lifetime girl.*

She brings me back when she leaves my lips. "And I love that you're always trying to be respectful, I really do. But I want to enjoy . . . *every* . . . *last* . . . *minute* . . . of my spring break," she says, playfully pressing into my chest with each word.

"You can have whatever you want."

"I can deal with that," she says before dipping back down to my lips and kissing me again.

Damn. I grip her waist and pull her into me with both hands. Forget my wrist.

She kisses me like there's no tomorrow.

I slide my hands down to her hips and have to stop myself from slipping them down even farther.

No tomorrow or the day after that or the day after that. She obviously doesn't understand what she's doing to me.

I stop and pull away. “Look,” I tell her, “I’m down with waiting. For real. As long as you want. I can wait until marriage if I have to. But this right here. This is making it real hard.”

Josie

"So we're just casually tossing out the word *marriage* now?" I ask, sitting all the way up. "Don't get me wrong, I love the idea that you're willing to wait to have sex. But *marriage* is a big word. I'm only eighteen. And you're only nineteen. So why even bring it up?"

"Damn," he says, looking surprised, "tell me how you really feel."

"Well, I get suspicious when it sounds like boys are overpromising," I say, thinking about the only two boyfriends I've ever had. David insisting we make a grand entrance to homecoming in a vintage Rolls-Royce convertible only to ditch me last minute for courtside Rockets tickets. And Keith telling me he loved me three days before Brittney saw him in the River Oaks District kissing another girl. I was pretty much done with boys after that.

"Look, I'm not promising anything," Shawn says calmly. "And obviously I'm not talking about now. But yeah, if we stay together . . . and things keep going up and up and up . . . and we start thinking we want to do life with each other . . . then why not?"

I study his face, open and sincere.

"I mean, how else you gonna get your five-six kids?

Gotta start poppin' them babies out young," he says, and playfully shakes my hips.

"Boy, shut up," I say, heart glowing inside my chest. Shawn is seriously making me believe that true love really exists. I start kissing him again.

After a minute or so, he squeezes my waist and stops. "Like, for real, Josie, maybe you should go put on some sweats before this other movie."

"I can do that."

When I come back, we decide that I should stay on my side of the love seat. I still drape my leg over his and put my head on his chest. But no straddling.

"I've always wanted to ride the London Eye," he tells me, gently rubbing my back as the giant Ferris wheel towers in the background of a high-speed car chase.

"Same."

"Maybe we can go one day."

Feeling his heart pound against the side of my face just as fast as mine, I say, "Yeah," and allow myself to wonder about our future together.

Shawn

"Josie! Renée! Riley! Get up!"

The sound of a woman yelling . . . bright lights . . . Josie shaking me. . . . *Shit, we feel asleep.*

"Just because we work late doesn't mean you get to break the rules! And on a school night?" Josie's mom says, stomping down the stairs toward us.

"But I can explain," Josie starts as we stand up and turn around.

"Good heavens!" her mom says, hands over her heart in what looks like half shock, half embarrassment. Her hair is imprinted with the ring of a cowboy hat, and her bandana-print blouse hangs loosely from her skirt. She starts tucking it in. "Sorry, I didn't realize that you two knew each other."

"My apologies, ma'am. We were watching a movie and fell asleep," I say.

"No, please, call me Cynthia," she says. "Lawrence is in the kitchen. Can we get you anything?"

"No, thanks, ma'am—sorry, Cynthia. I appreciate it. But it's really late. I should probably be on my way."

"Okay, I'll let Josie see you out, then. Be safe getting home tonight," she says, and starts back up the stairs.

"Thanks, goodnight."

"Whaaat?" Josie says after her mom leaves. Her eyes

are about as wide as they can be. "I know you're famous and all, but I didn't know you could work that kind of magic!"

I laugh.

"Seriously, I'm definitely keeping you around now. Even if it's only to deal with my mom."

Outside, on the doorstep, the early morning is quiet, dark, and cold. Must've dropped thirty degrees since earlier. The Houston weather can't decide what it wants to do.

"When can I see you again?" Josie whispers, shivering.

"Whenever you want," I say, my arms wrapped around her, wishing I could introduce her to Mom.

She stands on her tiptoes and tilts her chin up for a kiss.

I give it to her but keep it short. There are two cameras above the door. Not that I think her mom and dad are inside watching us, but I'm not about to push my luck.

I slowly back away from her, holding her hand until our arms stretch . . . only the tips of our fingers touching.

"Tomorrow," I tell her.

"Tomorrow."

Josie

At the breakfast table the next morning, I pour maple syrup over my pancake stack. Mom has a ramekin for her syrup because she can't stand anything soggy, and Daddy goes without. He's a savory person. The strawberries he put in the batter are enough.

"I still can't believe we didn't recognize Shawn," Mom says, and takes a bite of bacon. She's already dressed to perfection in a red, ruffle-necked blouse and bell-bottoms.

Mouth full, I don't reply. I need to leave for school in seven minutes, and I want to finish these pancakes. Plus, we already had this conversation.

"It was years ago. And we weren't in the best state of mind," Daddy says. Exact same response he had last night after Shawn left.

"You're right," she says, taking a sip of her coffee. "And I guess it's all happening the way God intended. It's such a blessing the way everything has fallen into place."

Now, that's new, I think, smiling in agreement.

"You and Shawn reuniting after all these years . . . it's just beautiful," she continues.

I lick the syrup off my bottom lip, honestly touched.

"And with Shawn and his friends running the stables

after the sale, you'll be able to see Strawberry whenever you want," Daddy says.

Wait? What!

"The situation could *not* be more perfect. You never know, maybe y'all will even get married one day," Mom teases.

Daddy stops eating and sets his wrists on the table, fork and knife sticking straight up in the air. "She's only eighteen, Cynthia."

"Come on. I said *one day*."

I laugh to play it off and fish for more information. "It's weird how the whole situation came together, isn't it?"

"I know, right," Mom says. "Who knew that talks about Shawn being the face of Riley Sauce—"

"That's the new product line y'all have been talking about, right?" I ask, casually picking up my orange juice as if I'm not having a complete and total meltdown inside.

"Yes, the barbeque sauces we plan to sell at the new restaurant. We've been in talks with Mr. Sterling for over a month about it. I may have mentioned the ranch a few times, but only so he would know that we weren't just city folks. Obviously, I had no idea he would introduce us to a buyer wanting to pay cash." She looks disgustingly happy with herself.

"Cash?" I let slip.

"Cash is king, sweetheart," Daddy says.

Here we go, I think, hearing a business lesson coming on.

"It's immediate, has no strings attached, and you don't

have to worry about chasing payments or dealing with loan approvals."

See, told you.

"It takes time for banks to approve loans," he continues. "And if something goes wrong, the buyer could end up with less money to offer, or worse, the whole deal could fall through. We might have to wait another week or so for the buyer to raise some capital, but after that, it should be a done deal. Clean and simple."

Clean and simple? I invited Shawn to the ranch! Introduced him to Mimi and Papa and Strawberry. I got snot on his white tee for crying out loud, which I'm pretty sure I actually did! Cry out loud, that is. And then this boy had the nerve to comfort me and tell me that he would help save the ranch when he was a freaking part of the deal? Oh, things are far from clean and simple.

Since Daddy's in teaching mode, I keep it together and ask, "So how did Shawn and his friends get factored into the deal?"

"I'm not sure. Shawn could probably tell you best. But I imagine it was a quid pro quo arrangement. His dad likely made the introduction to us in return for Shawn and his friends running the ranch. Happens all the time in business."

"They're supposedly starting some kind of horse training school and everything," Mom adds.

"Yeah, Sterling mentioned that," Dad replies.

Mom dips the tip of her pancake into the ramekin. "Teaching kids how to ride and care for horses . . . sounds amazing."

Really? You discourage me from working at the ranch my whole life, but now caring for horses sounds amazing? "I have to go," I say, standing up. I fight back my tears long enough to grab my backpack and get out.

"Have a good day!" Mom shouts as I open the front door.

Impossible.

I thought he was sooo different . . . sooo special, thought we might've been at the beginning of something truly beautiful. But he's just like the rest of them. No, worse. Because he convinced me that boys like him—sweet and protective and respectful and faithful and still funny and handsome, so handsome—actually exist.

I got you, he told me over and over again. But it was more like *Gotcha!*

I swear I'm done with boys. For real this time.

Forget the fantasy Shawn sold me. It wasn't real. And neither were the warm, cozy feelings I had for him. As a matter of fact, from now on you might as well call me Elsa because I'm going to be cold, ice cold, as in *Back up! Don't get too close!*

Maybe I'll make for a good princess after all.

Shawn

"Hey, this is Josie. I'm guessing it's you, Mimi. I'll call you back soon. Anybody else . . . what are you doing? Text me."

Straight to voicemail for the tenth time. And I've texted twice but she's not hitting me back.

I don't get it, I think, pressing the doorbell again. She's definitely here. I can hear music blasting, and her car is right there with the top down. It's not like I was late. I got here at four o'clock on the dot. Been out here looking crazy for damn near twenty minutes.

Maybe she's in the shower or something. I need gas anyway. So I decide to go fill up to give her more time.

But when I get back, the gate code isn't working anymore. I press one-eight-eight-zero again and again, thinking I must be tripping. Then I push the round silver button on the bottom of the intercom.

Two rings . . . loud rap music in the background . . . click.

Three rings . . . loud rap music in the background . . . click.

Six rings . . . loud rap music in the background . . . click.

Ring after ring after ring until I press the button to turn it off.

Could she be ghosting me?

No way.

But then I remember who I'm dealing with. How she left me standing there like a fool the night we met.

A monstrous hundred-foot wave of hurt blots out the sky and I throw my truck in reverse, trying to escape it. But I can't. The wall of pain comes crashing down and makes me pull over on the side of the road, right wrist throbbing because I keep forgetting not to use it.

Everything I thought she was, everything I thought we could be, gone. All the possibilities of what could have happened violently swirling around me—her parents flipping the switch after I left last night and her not standing up for me again . . . her back in the arms of the high school boyfriend she told me she didn't have . . . her thinking I'm not cute enough or rich enough or tall enough or funny enough or cool enough . . . good enough . . . not even worthy of a breakup conversation.

Tears running down my face, Rob's and Trey's words race across my mind.

Rob: You need to stop letting Josie play you.

Trey: Yeah, how many times you gon' let her leave you hanging?

Rob: Damn, dude, have some pride.

My boys tried to warn me, but I was too hardheaded. Too blinded by thinking Josie just might be the one. *Man*, I was trippin'.

I wipe my face with my bandage and put my car in drive. Head straight to Rob and Trey's house.

I haven't said a word about Josie since that day they came to see me ride. Called myself protecting our relationship so that it could grow. What a joke.

Josie

And now I feel guilty. Not because I blocked Shawn's number. Not because I didn't open the door when I knew he had to be cold standing on the porch in his white tee, pressing the bell over and over again. Not because I changed the gate code or even because I watched it all from the kitchen on my phone like a bad reality show. But because I ate the last of Daddy's dry roasted macadamia nuts while I did.

Shawn

"So let me get this straight: We can get paid a hundred K every year to run this horse school *and* get to train and film there for 44 Cowboys?" Trey says. He's sitting in his gaming chair, playing *Red Dead Redemption*, locs pulled back in a ponytail.

"This would be amazing. We could even link up with Grit and Grace Stables," says Rob. He's on the sofa beside me with his orange apron balled up in his lap. He still volunteers at the stables twice a week. "You know a lot of those kids have never been to a ranch or out in the country like that."

I stare at a man on the screen riding through the woods during a thunderstorm, trees bending and water splashing. *What was I thinking?* Telling them about Melvin's plan was the wrong move. What I really wanted to do was tell them about Josie, but driving to their house, I could already hear them:

Rob: So you mean to tell us that she ghosted you again?

Trey: No way! I'm shocked!

Rob: I can't imagine Josie ever doing something like that.

Trey: Bahahaha.

Rob: Come on, dude. It's not like we didn't warn you.

I couldn't handle getting clowned like that. Not after today, but I felt like I had to get something off my chest. My dad's debt . . . my stepmom and sisters . . . Melvin's plan . . . Josie . . . it was all sitting too heavy on me. But telling them about the deal just made everything worse.

"And I just got this new drone we can use for filming our moves!" Trey says, frantically pushing buttons to get his horse across a surging creek.

"You got a new drone?" Rob asks.

"Yeah, the internet needed to see your boy's craftmanship from all the angles."

"The internet doesn't need any more videos of you in that helmet with sparks flying—"

"Don't hate just because nobody wants to see you working at Home Depot."

"I go to work to make money . . . to get stock discounts and health benefits. Not to be all over the internet."

"What are you talking about? You post for Grit and Grace all the time."

"That's different. It's about getting the word out about the community center. Not me."

"And I make videos to get the word out about my skills. What's the difference?"

"Well, maybe if you spent less time on the videos and more time on the skills, you could've paid your half of the rent this month."

Trey pauses the video game and turns around. "Oh, you tryna take it there?"

"Man, y'all are like an old married couple around here,"

I say, and laugh, trying to ease the tension. "Anyway, y'all are talking like this is happening. It's not."

"But I could get some sick arial footage of us at the ranch," Trey says.

"And Charlie, Lil Love, and Super Fly would all be so much happier there," Rob adds. "Ms. Judy has a nice setup on her ten acres and all. But to be able to run around on open land is different."

"So different," Trey agrees. "Come on, Shawn. It's time for 44 Cowboys to get back in the game!"

"Y'all do realize that none of this can happen without me throwing my last ride, right?"

"Yeah, forget about it," Rob says.

Trey swivels around in his chair to face Rob. "Whatchu mean forget about it? Do you really want to be working at Home Depot the rest of your life?"

"That's not the point. Plus, I won't be. This job is temporary."

"Isn't that the same thing your dad used to say?"

Rob jumps up off the sofa, ready to fight.

"Come on, y'all. Chill . . . chill," I say, standing up.

Trey starts playing his video game again like he wasn't worried anyway. Yeah, whatever. He knows he don't want no smoke from Rob.

Rob sits back down, vein in his neck still popping out. He's stacked. Lifts weights with his dad before work every morning.

"Didn't you say Josie was rich anyway," Trey asks, sharpening an arrow in the game. "Can't her family just go buy themselves another ranch?"

"It doesn't work like that," I reply, thinking about how the ranch has been in her family for one hundred and fifty years, how sacred it feels from the moment you start up the long drive and see the great big sky stretching out over the land.

"Oh, here you go defending Josie again," Rob says.

"It's bigger than Josie," I say.

"Damn right it is," Trey says, focused on an approaching wolf. "Have you even thought about what this deal could do for us? It could literally change our lives, dude."

"And we've been your boys since day one."

I expect this kind of pressure from Trey, but from Rob too? We've been tight since the third grade when Mrs. Fisher teamed us up for the science fair. We'd seen each other on the bayou trail a few times before. Him with his dad and me with Mom, so we knew we had that in common. We studied the effects of different kinds of music on horse behavior. Discovered that reggae helped both Lil Love and Charlie relax while getting their hooves cleaned.

"Yeah, for real," Trey says. He moved into the neighborhood from South Dallas a year after Mom died. He loved horses as much as me and Rob, and it was nice to have someone around who wasn't so sad for me all the time. "What has Josie ever done for you?"

A flashback of her brushing her lips along my scar, kissing my wrist, and I push back, trying not to cry. "How about what she hasn't done? Well, she's not trying to guilt me into throwing a ride for one. And she doesn't make it seem like my life is easy all the time."

"That's just because she got money too," Rob says,

"Money doesn't make all of your problems disappear!" I yell, sick of their crap for real.

"It sure does make things easier, though," Trey says, a pack of wolves surrounding his character.

"Okay, I don't have to worry about food or rent, but y'all act like I'm not out here working for it. I ride bulls for a living! Two-thousand-pound beasts! Not many people are doing that. Do you know how much training it took to get where I am? A lot! And it takes even more to stay on top! And let's not even bring my injuries into this." I look down at my wrapped-up wrist that neither one of them has bothered to ask me about.

"I almost died!" I continue. "Remember that? Y'all act like that's nothing. Like I'm not risking my life every time I ride. Like everything I get just magically falls into my lap. That's why I can't even talk to y'all anymore!"

It's quiet for a few seconds. Trey looking down at the remote control, game paused, and Rob playing with the tie on his apron.

Rob speaks up first. "My bad. I didn't know you felt like that."

"Sorry, dude," Trey adds. "I guess we have been acting a little messed up."

"I appreciate it," I tell them. "And trust me, I'm down with doing business with y'all. But this ain't the way."

"You said the same thing about investing in the Blessing Loom, though," Rob says.

"That was a straight pyramid scheme," I tell him. "It wasn't even trying to disguise itself by selling any kind of product. They were just out here scamming people."

"No, I'm telling you. You could've made ten times your investment."

"How much money did you make, then?"

"I lost mine, but if you would've joined—"

"Then he would've lost his money too?" Trey says, and busts out laughing. "Come on, dude. Even I knew that was a scam."

"What are you talking about? You're the one who recruited me!"

Trey gives Rob a square smile as if saying, *Oops*, and starts playing his game again.

We keep talking, everybody taking the opportunity to air out their issues. Apparently, Trey wastes way too many paper towels. And Rob never mows the lawn or cleans up after himself. Leaves rings around the tub after his mineral soaks and sweaty shirts on the bathroom floor. Nasty.

I'm over here enjoying not having the heat on me, thinking about how happy I am to live alone when they accuse me of never trying to put them on.

"Y'all can't be serious," I say, but I'm not surprised. People have a way of conveniently forgetting the ways they mess up when they're trying to blame someone else. A perfect opportunity to remind them of the jobs I offered them right after we graduated. Transport and logistics manager for Rob, but he didn't want to be on the road, away from his parents all the time. And videographer for Trey, but he kept showing up late and then broke the first camera we bought trying to film himself doing a trick on Super Fly.

"Oh, yeah. That's right," Trey says, and laughs.

We order pizza and take turns playing each other in *Madden*. After handing out a few Ls, I leave, hating that I would still give anything to have it out and be back on track like this with Josie.

Josie

The next morning, I'm downstairs dressed for school by 6:09 a.m. I flip on the lights above the island and grab the bell pepper, eggs, onions, sun-dried tomatoes, cheese, basil, oranges, and strawberries from the fridge. Set everything on the counter in front of the window.

Outside, the pool glows blue in the darkness, and I stand still for a second, marveling at how good I feel.

I have Shawn to thank for that. He did me a huge favor, being a total fraud. See, I'd gotten way too comfortable, like *way*, and he gave me a much-needed reality check: there's nobody coming to save me.

But that's okay because I have a plan.

Shawn was right. The sale of the ranch is *not* a done deal. And if he thinks I'm going to let him and his friends and that stupid Donny boy take my family's land, then he has another thing coming.

I pull a knife from the magnetic strip and get to work.

Twenty minutes later, Daddy comes in. "Morning, sweetheart. What's all this?"

Slicing an orange in half, I say, "I know how busy you and Mom get during rodeo season. Thought I'd help out."

He eyes me suspiciously. "Is everything okay?"

I turn round. "Yeah, everything is fine." Then I grab the

first step of my plan off the island and hand it to him. "This is for you."

"'From Dust to Dreams,'" he says, reading the proposal cover. He flips the page and looks pleasantly surprised.

I resist smiling at my decision to put the numbers up front.

"I didn't realize that painting had appreciated so much."

"Yeah, it's not an exact figure. But the artist blew up a couple years ago after her work was featured in a Louis Vuitton ad. Horses and cowboys are fashionable now. A trend that I think is here to stay. But I'll let you read the rest."

"Thanks for the pro tip," he says, laughing under his breath. "Maybe me and your mom can open a restaurant to capitalize on that trend."

"Okay, fair. I guess I didn't need to put that in there. But the longevity of the trend ties into the historical element, which I touch on in the next section. It's part of the reason I argue the painting will keep appreciating," I say, and send the butcher knife through another orange.

"Understood," he says, and keeps reading. "Part of America's spirit [illegible] symbolic of love, hard work, and determination?" He cuts me another suspicious look.

"What?"

"I don't know. The food prep . . . this proposal . . . it's a little . . . surprising, that's all."

He's right, this isn't my usual MO. I can't exactly say that I'm the model of hard work and determination around here. Like, I make decent grades. As and Bs. And sometimes I'll clean my room before the housekeepers come, if it gets so messy that I can't find anything. But I don't help out a ton at home.

It's weird because I'm the complete opposite at the ranch. There, I cook, clean, haul hay, pick fruit, and generally do whatever needs to be done without Mimi and Papa even having to ask. When I was little, I must've heard *Everyone in the family needs to contribute* a million times. Now, helping comes naturally.

But at home, I've had a free pass for as long as I can remember. "I'm trying to do better," I finally say. "Is that really so hard to believe?"

"Of course not, sweetheart. And I appreciate it. I do. So this is really all about the painting?"

"Yes," I lie. It's not time for my next step just yet.

"But you know we would never sell that piece. Your mom knows how much you love it. I probably shouldn't tell you, but we were planning to give it to you for graduation. You really didn't have to go through all of this."

See, that's exactly why I haven't written a proposal in years. Okay, I might've also been lazy. But who'd feel like writing a ten-page paper every time they wanted something big when they knew they'd eventually get it anyway? Not I. I always got what I wanted in the end.

Until I didn't.

"I needed the practice anyway," I tell Daddy, slicing another orange. "It's not like I have any real work at school the rest of the year. Most teachers have already started playing documentaries."

"That's right, you *are* heading to college soon. It's important to stay sharp. Those term papers are no joke."

I don't tell him that college isn't part of my plan anymore. Baby steps. "How did I do?" I ask, and grab three short glasses from the cabinet.

His eyebrows squeeze together in confusion.

I place half an orange over the top of the silver dome of the juicer. "On the proposal . . . like what grade would you give me?"

He thumbs through the pages until the end. "It looks great. But I don't see anything about maintenance and storage. So maybe . . . an A minus."

I press the handle down hard, and juice spurts into the glass. "No, I talk about that under the Responsibilities Involved with Ownership section."

He flips through until he finds it. "I see," he says, looking surprised. "You should be proud of yourself, sweetheart. This is good work. Real good work."

"Thanks," I say, feeling a small sense of victory start to spread across my chest. But I know that that I'm nowhere near finished yet.

"I guess I better get started on these omelets. You'll need to get out of here soon," Daddy says. walking around the island to wash his hands.

And Mom will be down here any minute. Time for phase two. I press another orange and tell Daddy about how John from three houses down snuck his dad's Mercedes out and crashed it over spring break.

"Not the 300SL Gullwing," Daddy says, looking up at

me, horrified, as he sautés the vegetables.

"Yep, totaled it."

"Are you serious?"

I keep pressing. "Dead serious."

"Do you know how much that car was worth? Jim has to be losing his mind."

"Three million or something like that, right?" I ask, as if haven't done the research.

"Three point nine! And it had belonged to Jim's late father. Do you know he bought that car for seven grand when it first came out? That was Jim's baby. He only took it out once a month to keep everything in working order."

"Wow, it appreciated that much?" I ask, still playing dumb.

"Yes, its winged doors are very rare."

"But seven thousand to three point nine million? That's a lot for some doors," I say, to get him started on inflation.

"See, sweetheart, you have to remember how much the dollar devalues over time," he says, totally taking the bait.

And after nodding my way through his mini-lecture about the dollar's decoupling with gold, the massive amounts of government spending, and the importance of investing in things that grow faster than inflation, so your money doesn't shrink, I finally get a chance to drop my first big question. "It's kind of like the ranch, isn't it? Can you imagine what our ancestors would think if they knew the land that they literally slaved over, then sharecropped and bought for a hundred dollars, is now worth ten million?"

"They'd be dancing in their graves."

"Not if they knew we were selling it," I let slip. But I quickly get back on track and say, "Anyway, what do you think it'll be worth fifty or a hundred years from now?"

Daddy leans back against the sink and folds his arms across his chest. "I have no idea." After a minute or so of him standing there, staring into space, smoke starts rising from the pan.

I leave the juicer to flip the omelet.

"When did you learn how to do that?"

"I don't know. Probably when I was twelve or so. I make breakfast all the time for Mimi and Papa."

Daddy looks like I just told him I could fly.

This is the moment. Phase three. What this whole morning has been designed for. It's time to let him in on my master plan. "I've been wondering. Did you and Mom ever consider opening Riley Ranch on the ranch itself?"

"Well, your mom ruled it out because she thought it would be too rustic and too far," he says, but the way he's still standing there, with his arms crossed and that vacant look on his face, tells me he's rethinking that logic.

I slide the omelet onto a plate, throw more vegetables in the pan, and say, "It's only forty-five minutes from the city. And we could totally make it worth the drive. Have live music. Maybe s'mores around a campfire. We could even offer trail rides. And yes, it would be more rustic than our usual restaurants, but we could still make it really upscale."

"I don't know," he says, still in deep thought.

"People could make a day out of it if they wanted to. Maybe we could convert the old barn and stables into luxury locker rooms where people could shower and change before dinner. They're literally just sitting there collecting dust," I say, trying to contain my excitement.

Daddy doesn't say anything.

"Well, the last part could come later, or not at all. Just throwing out ideas."

Mom walks into the kitchen in a long black denim dress and her yellow diamond necklace. "Good morning."

Placing the last orange on the juicer, I say, "Morning."

Daddy straightens up and pours more whisked eggs into the pan. Then he turns to me and says, "I'm going to need a proposal ASAP."

Mom grabs the kettle and laughs. "Yeah, good luck with that."

Then while Mom is filling the kettle with water, Dad gives me a look as if to say, *This stays between us for now.*

And I look back like, *Oh, you don't even have to tell me!*

Mom is going to have an absolute fit when she finds out about my plan. She's had her mind set on selling the ranch for years. Somewhere along the way, she got the idea stuck in her head that the opportunity for growth can only happen in the city among the bougie types. That manual labor is a waste of energy for anyone with brains or talent. That sophistication and prestige is everything.

It's not.

But convincing her that she's completely wrong isn't going to be easy. Exactly why I needed to secure backup. This morning was a success, but I can't throw my hat in the air just yet. I still have a lot of work ahead.

Shawn

I squint to adjust from the bright sun to the darkness inside. Thick cigarette smoke grips my throat, and I cough before I call out, "Dad?"

No cute, little sparkly shoes by the door. No women's heels or sneakers either. I slide off my boots and head to the back, trying to shake off this weird feeling that I'm in a stranger's house.

The plants are gone. The toys, usually in bins and scattered across the floor, are gone. The Princess Tiana and Moana fluffy blankets are gone. The colorful books that once sat in messy stacks in the display case are gone. The finger paintings on the fridge are gone. Black Jesus is gone.

Man, this isn't Shelly's usual I'll-be-at-my-Mom's-until-you-get-your-act-together move. She's left him for real this time.

The drapes and blinds along the backside of the house are closed. I twist the long plastic rod on the closest window in the breakfast room, ready to let in some much-needed light and fresh air.

"Leave it," Dad's voice calls from behind me.

Makes me jump a little.

I turn around. "My bad . . . didn't see you back there."

"How'd you get in?" he asks gruffly from the large leather recliner in the far corner of the living room, empty beer cans littering the carpet around him. Shelly hated that chair. He must've brought it in from the garage.

"I still," I say, coughing, "I still have my key."

"Well, won't be of use much longer."

"Look, you gotta let me open some windows. I can barely breathe," I tell him, raising the blind. I unlock the window and slide it up. When I don't hear a protest, I open two more windows and the drapes in the living room. "There, that's better" I say, and turn around.

But it's not.

"Dad." I sigh, staring at him slumped in his chair, wondering how he let himself go like this. He looks more broken than I've ever seen him.

His eyes are bloodshot red and gazing straight ahead as if unaware of the cigarette burning between his fingers. His cheeks are hollow. And he's still in his boots and jeans but has his shirt off—muscles sagging on his thin frame.

I can't help but stare at his chest, etched with a hundred jagged scars from the countless falls, tramplings, and gorings. It's like a history of his brutal career. From the surgeries to repair his broken ribs and arms to his torn rotator cuffs and punctured lungs, he's been through hell.

He presses his cigarette into the cupholder in the armrest. "You think you're better than me, don't you?"

"What? Dad, no." I go kneel beside him.

He smells like he hasn't showered in days. "Who do you think taught you how to ride?"

I wish he'd look at me. "You did."

"And who do you think paid for all of your equipment and gear and entry fees and travel?"

"You."

"And what about all your clothes and meals?"

"Dad, you. And I'm grateful. I really am," I say, already knowing where he's going with this.

He finally glances at me. "You sure don't act like it."

"I mean, if you're talking about Melvin's deal with the ranch, I can't be a part of that," I say. "But I can help you with your debt. How much do you owe?"

He goes back to staring ahead into space.

"Fifty?"

He doesn't answer.

"A hundred?"

He still won't answer.

"Damn, two hundred thousand?"

He balls his bony fingers and slams his fists into the arms of the chair. "It's not enough! I need you to do the deal!" he shouts, bits of spit flying in my face.

I wipe it off with the bottom of my white tee and go stand beside the fireplace. Looking out of the window at Shelly's dying plants on the back porch, I think about how the man who raised me would never ask me to do something like this. Never in a million years.

But he also never would've gambled himself into a massive hole. And now that he's there, I don't know what to do. I don't want him to lose his house and wife and kids. *Family is everything.* He's the one who taught me that.

"There has to be another way," I finally say.

"You owe me," he says, gripping the arms of the chair.

I can't even argue with him. It doesn't matter how much money he's made off my contracts or the side deals or all the times I've paid off his debts. There's no way I could ever repay him for stepping up to the plate to raise me.

"I just . . . I don't know," I say, head spinning, thinking maybe the good it could do for him and my friends would balance it all out.

"Well, know this—you would be nothing if it wasn't for me. I took you in when nobody would. Your drug-dealing auntie in Beaumont didn't have time for you. And you better bet your real daddy didn't want you. He already had a wife and kids."

His words explode through me, and I grab onto the mantel, feeling my whole life crumbling. My mom told me my real dad died from a stroke before I was born.

"You're old enough to know the truth, son."

"I'm not your son!" I yell, tears streaming down my face, hating him.

And now he's up and his hand is on my back. "It'll be okay," he says.

I shrug him off. "Okay? Apparently I have brothers and sisters who don't know I exist! A father who's alive but wanted no part of me! A dead mother who . . . who . . . I don't even want to think about it!" And now I'm free-falling into a dark pit of hurt and confusion. "I gotta go," I say, and head for the door.

"Wait!" he says, following me.

But I keep it moving.

"I was just trying to get you to see that you have to do the deal."

Man, I can't believe this dude.

"You don't understand, I've already committed you," he presses, still on my heels. "Other people besides Melvin are involved. And these folks don't play. You have to do this! You hear me?"

I open the door, the rush of sun and warmth making me feel like I'm stepping into a different world.

"You hear me?" he repeats.

I slam the door and get the hell out of there.

But his words follow me inside my truck, back to my house, and into my bed, where I cry like a baby for hours. Where I hold the picture from my nightstand: Mom beside me as I kneel on Lil Love, hands in the air. Where I stay until it's pitch-black and I'm hungry and have to pee but feel too heavy to even get out of bed.

I need someone to talk to.

Not my boys. No way. I swear if they opened their mouths one time to say something sideways about Mom, that would be the end of us. Crack one dumb joke and I'd lose my mind. I can't take them right now.

So I call Josie. Straight to voicemail. Must still have me blocked. I don't know what I'm doing calling her anyway.

Yesterday, she made it clear that she doesn't give a damn about me.

So I hit up Tara. She may not be perfect, but she's always there.

Josie

I spin around in my desk chair, again and again, thrilled at my progress. I'm nearly finished with this proposal. I worked on it after school yesterday until I conked out at three a.m. Got a four-hour power nap and a mug of Mom's coffee before jumping back in this morning. Yes, it's Wednesday, but I convinced Daddy to go along with me playing sick. It's like, what's more important: school or saving the land that's been in our family for five generations?

Now it's almost midnight and I'm exhausted. But I need to make this proposal so perfect that it'll be impossible to reject. Things are coming down to the wire.

The plan is to get Daddy's stamp of approval tomorrow. Take it to Mimi and Papa's on Friday. And spend the weekend at the ranch convincing them to call off their meeting with the buyer, which is set for Monday. I'm praying that when Mimi and Papa read this and find out that Daddy is on board with helping to secure funding, it'll be a wrap.

My phone buzzes and I stop spinning. Dizzy, I see a text pop up.

Billie
Permission to go off?

Billie's at the rodeo carnival with her friends from school. It's their spring break this week. Knowing her, she's probably leaned too far over the ring toss line again. Last time, the operator refused to give her a Squishmallow even though she landed a bottle. Let me tell you, she had a fit.

I laugh, thinking, *Always trying to pop off on somebody. You need to relax and stop trying to cheat*, before I pick up my phone and open her message.

In my face: Shawn and Tara side by side on the Ferris wheel, looking like they're meant to be.

A rush of heat flashes up my chest and cheeks. *I knew it!*

Me
ABSOFREAKINGLUTELY

Shawn

A girl in a big turquoise beaded hat runs up on me as soon as I step off the Ferris wheel with Tara. Wait, it's Josie's cousin. "You lying, backstabbing son of a bitch!"

I stand there, stunned, her words echoing through me.

"The nerve of you to come to the ranch! What were you doing? Scoping it out?" she screams in my face. "Are you seriously telling me that there was no other way for you and your boys to get what you wanted than to take our family's land?"

Horror flashes through me as I realize Josie must've found out about Melvin's plan. Wondering how, I try to explain, "Billie, look—"

"Wait . . . we can't forget that you get your face on the Riley barbeque sauce too. Whoop-de-do!"

"My face on what?" I say, before vaguely remembering the man I use to call *Dad* mentioning something about a sauce line a few weeks back. "I didn't—"

"And now you're out here with another girl on top of everything else?"

"No, Tara is just—"

"*Oh, he's not like other boys*, she kept telling me. *He's such a gentleman.* But you're nothing but a two-timing scammer!"

"Oh, hell no," Tara says, stepping between me and Billie. "First of all, you need to back up. Second of all, you don't know what you're talking about."

Yesterday, I broke down and told Tara everything. She held me and let me cry. Stayed over and didn't try to make a move the whole night. Went home this morning but still texted to check on me all day. Insisted I get out of the house tonight. Been a good friend.

"Oh, so you have girls fighting your battles now. You're more of a coward than I thought."

"Look, I think it's best you get to stepping," Tara says, staring her down.

"Or what?" Billie asks, still in her face.

"Oh, trust, you don't want none of this."

And she's right. Billie might talk tough, but according to Josie, it's all bark, no bite. I've seen Tara's bite, and it ain't pretty. The last thing I need is for Tara to give Josie's cousin a beatdown. "Ladies," I say, gently tugging Tara's arm, "how about we all just go our separate ways."

"Fine," Tara says.

But Billie's not done. "You're lucky he pulled you away!"

Tara doesn't let it slide. She flirtatiously glides her hand up my arm to my shoulder, where she rests her head. "I sure am."

Josie

After an hour in bed with the lights out, trying not to think about Shawn and that stupid Tara girl, I grab my phone and scroll. Look at:

Hannah making a duck face in the school's bathroom mirror.

So basic.

Jabari at his desk, reading his acceptance email from Duke, his mom in tears.

Aw, go, Jabari.

My baby cousin and his chunky little rolls.

Kisses.

An ad with a lady spraying deodorant on her privates.

Eww, go take a shower.

A montage of photos posted by yet another senior cheerleader. Caption: **Forever our squad.**

If I have to see that video one more time.

Kaia spiking a volleyball in some big tournament she's missing school for in Florida.

She's a beast!

A bright number one pops up in the top right corner of my screen. A new message. Probably another version of that dance Sage wants me to learn with her. I swear she thinks dancing is the cure for everything. I open it and read:

Shawn
You practically . . . now

My stomach shoots up into my heart, and I close the app. I didn't even think to block his DMs. We've rarely communicated on Instagram. Shared a few horse videos, but that's it.

I slide my phone back on the nightstand, determined to keep my cool and ignore him. I don't know why he's reaching out anyway. Clearly, he's moved on. Billie said Tara was all over him.

But I can't help but wonder what the rest of his message says. So I grab my phone, get back to the app, and stare at the first two words.

Shawn
You practically . . . 3 min

A mistake because I'm already heating up. *What? Please tell me what I practically did*, I silently scream at him. *Let you into my entire world?*

Shawn
You practically . . . 4 min

I roll over on my back, hold the phone above my face, and stare into the bright light. *I practically? I practically trusted you with everything!*

Shawn
You practically . . . 5 min

I throw the covers off and slide my phone back on the nightstand again, but that doesn't help. In the darkness, my anger turns soft. *I swear I hate you,* I think, desperate to stop the tears, but they stream down my face and puddle into my ears. *I practically loved you.*

Shawn
You practically . . . 8 min

I'm just going to read his message so I can stop thinking about him and get to bed. No way I'm responding.

Shawn
You practically made up your mind that I'm shady. And I can see why but I'm not. I guess I should've told you about Melvin's plan, but I was trying to protect you. Melvin is dangerous and I figured the less you knew the better.

Either way I'm sorry.

But the deal was never going to happen. I didn't even find out about it until after I got home from the ranch that night. That's why my dad was blowing me up. I don't even call him that anymore. Whatever . . . the point is I made it clear from the jump that I wanted no part of the deal. You have to trust me.

All I ever wanted to do was protect you Josie. And protect the ranch.

Do you really think I could go out there and meet Mimi and Papa and Strawberry and Ollie and then try to take it behind your back? I'm not that dude. You know I'm not.

And I'm sure Billie had plenty to say about Tara but she's just a friend. I've been going through a lot. And she's been there.
That's all.

I'm still riding with you.

And only you.

If you let me.

Please talk to me.

Shawn

Josie
Seen just now
. . .

The three bouncing dots disappear, and I stare at my screen, waiting for them to come back, praying for her to respond.

Josie

Seen 2m ago

Seen 3m ago

Seen 4m ago

Seen 5m ago

Seen 6m ago

Seen 7m ago

Seen 8m ago

Seen 9m ago

Seen 10m ago

Seen 16m ago

Seen 22m ago

Seen 28m ago

Seen 33m ago

Seen 47m ago

Seen 1h ago

Seen 2h ago

Seen 8h ago

Seen 9h ago

Seen 10h ago

Seen 13h ago

Seen 14h ago

Seen 15h ago

Seen 16h ago

Seen 17h ago

Seen 18h ago

Seen 19h ago

Seen 20h ago

Seen 21h ago

Seen 22h ago

Seen 1d ago

Seen 2d ago

Josie

"Josie, wake up! Wake up! The horses are out!" Mimi yells frantically, shaking me from sleep.

"What?" I sit up, heart racing, disoriented. For a second, the room turns bright, and I wonder why until I hear a massive *BOOM*. The rain banging on the roof. The howling wind.

Mimi clutches her robe. "Some prowlers let the horses out! Your papa and George are saddling up to bring them back in."

"No, Papa can't! He could hurt himself!"

"He doesn't have a choice. Folks trust us to keep their horses safe."

I jump out of bed. "Are you listening to yourself? We need to stop him."

"But Strawberry is loose too."

"I'll find her." I grab my jeans off the floor and slip them on underneath my nightgown.

"Josie, you don't understand. Whoever opened the stables could still be around."

"I'll be fine," I insist, rushing out of my room.

"They could be dangerous!" she cries, on my heels.

A tinge of fear in my chest and it hits me. This is retaliation for Mimi and Papa backing out of the deal.

Pissed, I shove my feet into my boots by the front door. "I'm going!"

"But Josie—"

"Mimi, we don't have time for this!"

"Okay, but you're taking George." She concedes. "And where's your phone?"

"Ugh," I say, picturing it on my nightstand.

"Go get it!"

"But Papa—

"Look, I'll stop him. Just go get your phone and the Glock and meet me in the stables," she says.

I pause, a little surprised.

"Hopefully you won't have to use it, but you need to be prepared."

I nod. I'm better with a rifle, but I can shoot a Glock just fine.

She heads out and I rush back to my room for my phone. Text Billie on the way to the safe. Mr. George is not as old as Mimi and Papa, but he's still slow at his age. He won't cut it. But even the addition of Billie won't be enough to wrangle all the horses in a storm this bad, especially with the risk of running into Melvin and his men.

My mind goes to Shawn. But it's been two days since I left him on read. I don't know if I should call him.

In a split second, my heart answers, *Yes*.

Shawn

I'm flying down this country road, trying to get to Josie.

"Didn't realize this old thing had so much get-up-and-go," Rob says. Trey is in the back. When Josie called in a panic about the horses being out and Melvin likely being behind it, I knew I needed backup.

"Don't sleep," Trey says. "Remember he had that V8 put in. Truck still needs some rims, if you ask me, but it ain't no punk. Cranks out four hundred horsepower."

It actually packs more like four hundred and thirty, but I don't correct him. Gotta stay focused on the road. The rain is coming down in sheets.

"Isn't it crazy that we still measure a car's power in terms of how much a real horse could pull?" Rob asks. "It's basically like this truck has four hundred horses crammed under the hood."

"Not really," Trey says, and laughs.

Rob shakes his head. "Whatever, dude."

Two bright lights ahead and I slow down. As we get close, I see flashes of whirling silver spokes in my beams. "Yo, that's Melvin," I say, holding my ground. I refuse to let him push me off the road.

It's a Charger, not a Cadillac. But it has the same ugly

metallic orange paint. "Hold up, that's not Melvin. That's Donny."

We creep by slow, mean-mugging them.

"They don't want no smoke," Trey yells once we pass.

"Nope!" Rob agrees. "Which is exactly why them fools are headed back to the highway."

Hoping they're right, I glare at the red taillights in my rearview. Watch them get farther and farther away, until they disappear in the storm.

Josie

Mud splatters my face as Mr. George and I corral two more skittish horses. I should've taken the raincoat Mimi tried to give me before we left. My nightgown and jeans are soaked, clinging to my skin.

"Aye-yo!" Mr. George shouts, and the barn's double doors swing out.

The first person I see is Shawn, standing between the stalls with Rob, Trey, Mimi, and Papa. Eyes steady, holding mine.

Everything inside me melts and I'm swimming in a pool of relief and guilt. Not only did he come, but he brought reinforcements.

I swing down off Cassidy.

But beside me, Mr. George is slow. He lands hard, his waterlogged boots squelching as they hit the rubber mat. "Well, we've caught the easy ones. Now comes the hard part."

"I think we can take it from here," I tell him.

He wipes the mud off his weathered face. "I can get back out there if you need me to."

"No, we're good."

"Josie." Shawn's voice cuts through the chatter of his friends as he walks toward me. "What do you need us to do?"

Mimi holds a raincoat in front of me like a makeshift curtain. "I'll see if I can find more gear for everybody," she says, giving me a look before rushing off again.

I slip on the coat. Guess my nightgown was more see-through than I realized. Suddenly embarrassed, I fumble with the zipper as I try to hold the jacket together.

"Here," Shawn says, reaching to help, fingers brushing mine. He eases the zipper up and meets my gaze at the top.

"Thanks for coming," I tell him, staring into his eyes. "I'm really sorry I didn't respond. I was still so confused."

"All good . . . we can talk about that later," he says, and waves. He winces a tiny bit, but I still catch it.

"Your wrist!" I'd forgotten all about it.

"It'll be fine."

"But you have to ride next week. There's no way you should be—"

"Look, don't worry about all that. The ranch is what matters right now."

I stare at him, wondering how I ever doubted him.

"We saw Donny and his boys heading out on our way in. So at least we don't have to worry about them. What's the latest with the horses?"

"We still have fourteen on the loose. We already brought back the ones who were nearby. The rest are probably in the back pasture or by the creek."

"What about Strawberry? Have you found her yet?"

"No."

"We'll find her."

"Papa," I call out, "okay for Shawn to take Henry?"

"Of course," Papa says, walking closer. "This black stallion may be old but he's sturdy and won't scare for nothing."

"Okay, thanks." I think about the calmest horses we brought back in. "Mr. George, can you please saddle up Bandit, Ranger, and Ginger? I know Billie is going to—"

"You know Billie what?" my cousin says, walking into the barn. She lowers the hood of her yellow raincoat and begins to shake out her sleeves. "Girl, you owe me. Do you see my hair? I just got a blowout yesterday—wait, what is he doing here?"

"He's here to help," I tell her.

"Oh my gosh, Josie, please don't tell me you're drinking this fool's Kool-Aid again. After everything he—"

"Billie Adele Colton," I say, pulling one from Mom's playbook. "We don't have time for this. Trust me, we're lucky to have him and his friends here to help."

"Humph, you might think you're lucky," she says under her breath.

I ignore her. "As I was saying, Dalilah is just as jumpy as Strawberry in bad weather. You should take Ginger instead."

"I don't know. I—"

"Mr. George is already getting a saddle on her," I say firmly. And then louder and stronger to the rest of the group, "We're looking for fourteen more horses. We have a lot of ground to cover. We should split up. Shawn and I can head to the back pasture, and Billie, Rob, and Trey, y'all can head west to the river. Billie can lead the way."

They all nod and we move fast. Papa and Mr. George

helping to tighten the girths and adjust the bridles. Mimi handing out ponchos and stuffing saddlebags with extra halters and lead ropes. The horses stomping and shifting. All of us sensing the big mission ahead.

Shawn

"Easy, boy." Josie's soothing voice floats through the darkness.

The white stallion snorts but takes a shaky step forward out of a patch of trees and drops his head. Man, Josie has a gift. Watching her calm and coax these horses has been unreal. She's out here making it look easy. Let me tell you, it's not. I haven't been able to get a rope around a single neck.

"Good boy," she says.

I shift in the saddle, trying to keep my three steady. One of the mares shuffles sideways and I tighten my grip. The storm has eased off, but the horses are still wound up, stomping their hooves in the mud and jerking their heads with every grumble from the clouds. They know this storm ain't over. We need to get back before it starts up again.

Josie seems to realize the clock is ticking too, because she says, "Let's move," and clicks her tongue.

I follow her lead, one horse on each side and one trailing behind. We fall into a slow rhythm, Josie letting out soft reassurances now and again to keep everyone calm, including me. I'm used to riding Lil Love and all, but trying to ride while guiding multiple horses in a storm is no joke. Especially with my sore wrist.

We cross a shallow dip where the mud gets slick and Henry slips, throwing his head back and rolling his eyes. I squeeze my knees and hold the reins steady as if to say, *Don't even think about it*. If he bolts, they'll all scatter, and we'll be back at square one. "You're okay," I tell him in a soft voice. He fights me for a couple more seconds but settles. "Atta boy. Now, let's keep it moving."

Another rumble and I glance up, praying the storm holds out until we make it back. If the horses are doing all this flinching and grunting now, I can't imagine how they'll be if the rain starts coming down hard again.

We press on and I catch a glint off the old windmill's silver blades. Hear a faint creak in the wind from their spin. The lights from the house and stables seem to be getting brighter with each step.

Almost there.

The horses ease a bit like they know too.

When we finally make it, Mimi, Papa, and Mr. George guide the horses inside and back to their stalls.

I hop down off Henry, heart hammering like I'm sitting on a rank bull in the chute.

"Dude, I'm telling you, if I had my GoPro, we could've made a movie," Trey says to Rob and Billie, standing over by the tack room. He must be feeling the adrenaline too, because he's hype. "It was like the Wild, Wild West out there." He turns to Billie. "The way you were roping those horses! You would've definitely been the hero. I would've been your trusty sidekick." He grins wide before cocking his head and giving Rob a look. "But you? I don't know what you would've been. How does Billie lead four, I bring back three . . . and you just one? An NPC, for sure," he says, and laughs.

"Y'all didn't find her?" Josie yells in their direction. She's standing in front of the first stall, where *Strawberry* is etched on the brass doorplate.

Busy paying attention to Trey, nobody answers.

"Where is Strawberry?" Josie shouts.

Billie turns back. "We didn't see her anywhere."

Mimi emerges from a nearby stall and puts her arm around Josie, but I can't tell what she's saying from here.

Josie stomps off toward me. "We gotta go back out."

Still holding Cassidy's and Henry's reins, I take a deep breath, trying to get my mind right.

"Strawberry and Ollie are still missing," she continues.

"I told you that y'all need to wait until it dies down again," Mimi says, right behind her.

She's right. From the banging on the roof, it sounds like the whole sky is unloading right now.

"We can't!" Josie says.

"Just wait five minutes," Mimi pleads.

"We don't have five minutes," Josie snaps back.

"No horse is worth your neck," Mimi says.

Josie is looking at Mimi like she just slapped her.

"Who are we going to take?" I cut in, trying to dial back the tension and buy more time. I'm not gonna lie, I'd rather wait for the storm to ease up too. "Henry and Cassidy are too tired."

"They're all tired," Josie replies, taking Cassidy's reins.

I wish Papa could help settle Josie down, but he's in the hospital stall with Mr. George tending to one of the mares we brought in with a gash in her leg.

"Shawn's right," Mimi says firmly. "I can put saddles back on Ranger and Bandit. Cassidy and Henry have done their part for tonight. They need to rest."

"Fine," Josie replies, and then to the rest of the group: "Anybody else coming?"

A look of horror passes over Trey's face before he grabs his shoulder and says, "I totally would, but I don't think I can."

I roll my eyes. After all that talk, dude wants to fake being hurt.

Rob doesn't bother with an excuse. "Sorry. It's too dangerous out there now."

At least he's being honest. I can respect that.

"Well, y'all aren't about to leave me!" Billie says, and walks over to join us.

A wall of rain beats down on our heads as we ride out of the barn.

Josie shouts something but I can't hear her.

I slide the hood of my poncho down. At this point, I'm soaked through anyway.

"Yah!" Josie yells before snapping the reins. And she's off.

Billie burns out after her.

I'm right behind them.

As we rip across the field, they act like they don't notice that we're riding deeper into the madness—thunder booming louder, wind and rain whipping harder, and lightning closing in by the second. It's like these girls have no fear.

But I do. I suck in a deep breath, trying to keep it together. We have a long way to the pasture that Strawberry and Ollie love. Last trip out, nobody made it that far.

When we reach the woods, I'm relieved to be able to slow down and steady myself. But Josie and Billie keep charging ahead, weaving in and out of trees like it's nothing.

"I'm gonna head toward the river," Josie shouts over her shoulder as we near the far edge of the woods. "Y'all make sure Strawberry hasn't made it to the road."

"Wait!" I yell. We need to stay together.

But before I know it, Josie's off again.

Josie

A streak of lightning briefly turns night into day, and I see something moving up ahead.

Another flash shows Ollie, pacing in front of the river, his dark, slick coat shining.

A panicked whinny pierces through the pounding rain, and I pick up the pace until the sound of rushing water fills the air.

"Whoa, whoa!" I shout, shifting back my weight, giving a light tug to the reins, and easing the pressure from my legs. Bandit slows to a halt. I hop down and tie him to a nearby tree before making my way over to Ollie, slowly, careful not to frighten him more than he already is. "It's okay, boy. It's okay."

He's still frantically walking back and forth—mane plastered to his neck, nostrils flaring, and eyes wide with fear.

I need to get him away from the river. It's flooded over the banks and swirling with broken branches and limbs. I reach out, but he tosses his head. "Easy, boy," I say softly, and lower my hand. "It's me, Josie," I remind him. "I'm just trying to get you out of here."

His ears swivel back, and he slows a bit.

"That's it." I inch closer and gently stroke his neck.

He's trembling all over and, even in the rain, his body is steaming hot.

"You're okay, you're okay." I try to soothe him.

But he stomps and jerks his head toward the water. Then he lets out another whinny—sharp and urgent—as if trying to tell me something.

"What happened, boy?" I ask him, a wave of worry rising inside me. "Where's your sister?"

Shawn

Up ahead, Billie's yellow raincoat is getting closer and closer. "Do you see that?" she shouts when I catch up.

I don't know how she's making out anything in this downpour. "See what?"

"Look! There!" she says, jabbing her arm into the darkness.

I finally see a faint light in the distance. "What? The neighbor's house?"

"No, the neighbor is miles down the road. Let's ride that way to check it out."

"Okay," I yell, and we keep riding—rain spanking us from one angle and then, as if switching hands, hitting us from another—until twin white dots appear.

Billie slows down and shouts, "Headlights!"

"Why is the car just sitting there?" I ask, already coming up with the worst possible reason.

She must be thinking the same thing because she yells, "Yah!" and burns out.

I lean forward on Ranger, and he takes off after her, slipping before catching himself. I pat him on the neck. "That's my boy. Can't let us go out like that." He's been a beast the whole night. It ain't easy keeping your balance in a storm.

We find our rhythm again, rain stinging my face, everything a blur except Billie's jacket and the faint twin beams ahead.

Then a bright, jagged crack in the sky lights everything up. The wire fence. The metallic orange Charger on the other side of it. *What are they still doing here?*

"Wait!" I yell, but Billie can't hear me. She's too far ahead.

I squeeze Ranger between my knees and lean forward, chest pressing against his long neck. He picks up speed, and in another flash, I see a dude standing at the fence with some big red bolt cutters. Of course. These fools are cutting holes in the fence to let the horses out. Probably been doing it around the whole property. I hope Strawberry and Ollie haven't gotten out.

Mud starts flying back into my face, and I guide Ranger to Billie's side. "Wait!" I yell again.

But she's still not listening. It takes the fence coming up on us to finally slow her down.

"We need to go back!" I shout. "That's Donny and his boys!"

"The same Donny who attacked Josie and let out the horses tonight?"

"Yeah, we drove past them on the way in. There are at least three of them. We gotta get out of here!"

"Oh, hell, no!" she says, sliding off Ginger. She ties the horse to a tree.

"Billie, we can't take them by ourselves!" But the next thing I know, my boots are in the mud going after her, and we're running right at these fools.

Josie

I drop Ollie's reins and slide down the side of the bank into the cold current. "Strawberry!" I yell, clawing at the mud to keep my balance. Can't help her if I get swept away.

She's on her side, pinned underneath a huge live oak branch in the middle of the raging river. Three legs thrashing, one hanging broken as she struggles to keep her head above water.

"Hold on, girl! Hold on!"

She lets out a wild cry, eyes wide, terrified.

I rush in, water quickly rising from my knees to my chest. The strong current clutches at me, trying to drag me down, and I hear Mimi's words, *No horse is worth your neck*. But there's no way I'm leaving Strawberry out here.

"I'm here, girl. I'm here," I say, lifting her head out of the water.

Her chest heaves and she snorts hard, water spraying from her nostrils before she pulls in a wheezy breath.

"You're okay, girl. . . . Everything's okay."

But her body is trembling, and her eyes are rolling with fear.

I gently stroke her forehead. "No worries, girl. You're okay."

She finally looks at me and calms a bit.

"There's my girl. Hey, Strawberry," I say softly, silently panicking about the river rising around her head. Even though the rain has let up, the water is still surging downstream. I need to move the branch.

When I let go, she immediately starts thrashing again.

I press my hands into the wet wood and push and push and push. But it only sinks me deeper into the mud. "Come on!" I yell, and wedge my boots against a boulder. I push again, harder, even harder, shoulders burning, heart pounding. But it doesn't budge. I wrap my arms around it and try pulling, but there's no use. It's just too heavy.

Strawberry snorts desperately.

I rush back to her, praying that this is all a bad dream. That it's not really happening.

She shakes her head wildly, wheezing and snorting.

"Help!" I scream over the roaring river but there's only Ollie, still pacing frantically in front of the trees.

Strawberry thrashes, nostrils flaring and quivering as she forces out water and fights for breath.

"Help! Somebody, please help!" I cry, trying to keep her nose above water. But I can't. It's rising too fast.

She's drowning.

Shawn

"Let's go!" I yell.

But Billie's not finished. "I *said* get the hell off our property!" She's screaming at the top of her lungs with a pointed finger in the air.

"Don't worry, it won't be yours for long," Donny shouts back, and laughs. He's sitting in his car with the door open while his boys do all the work. The rain has stopped.

"Get away from our fence!" she yells at the two dudes as if they didn't hear her the first ten times.

"Look, we're just doing our jobs," one of them says as he cuts the wire. Dang, that's Pete! Back in the day, he used to be a good calf roper. He was cool . . . always shared his snacks. Don't know how he got mixed up with Donny.

Billie walks closer to the fence. "You call this a job?"

The quiet dude, holding the fence steady, takes the cigarette out of his mouth and calmly says, "Can somebody shut this bitch up?"

I don't have a clue who he is, but the tattoos covering his face, neck, and knuckles are telling me all I need to know.

"Bitch? Who you calling a bitch!" Billie shouts, and rushes at him.

I go after her and pull her back by the arm. It would be different if it was just Donny. But there's no way I can protect her against all three of them.

"That's right. You better get your girl, Shawn. Over here acting all hard. She needs to take her ass back to the crib," Donny says.

"Make me!" Billie yells, breaking free and going at him again. "You're clearly okay with hitting girls, you coward!"

"You're right, I am," Donny says, stepping out of the car. Before I know it, he's charging through the fence.

Billie jumps back.

I sprint to get between them. "Go!" I tell her. "Get help!"

Josie

"You'll forever be my favorite girl," I tell Strawberry, tears surging down my face.

She's shaking uncontrollably. Eyes wide and glassy.

I kiss her on the forehead. "I love you so much."

Her nostrils and lips twitch.

"More than you'll ever know," I say, heart howling.

Foam begins to seep from her mouth.

"I'm so sorry," I whisper, and squeeze the trigger. Wailing, I throw my arms around her lifeless head.

Down.

Down.

Down I sink into a raging spiral of darkness.

No bottom in sight.

A panicked whinny, followed by violent sloshing near the bank, yanks me out. I turn to see that Ollie is in the creek.

I shove the gun back into my shoulder holster. "No, Ollie, no!" I scream, fighting through the water, aching with each step I take away from Strawberry.

He lunges forward.

"Stop!" I cry, rushing to his side. No bridle, so I grab him by the muzzle, fingers digging into the wet hair around his nostrils, and pull with all my strength.

He jerks his head away and lets out a loud whinny in protest.

"Easy, boy. Come on, now. I can't lose you too."

But he's not hearing it. He stumbles farther into the swirling river.

"Please," I beg, and push his shoulder, trying to turn him.

He swings his head around, ears pinned back, and snaps at me.

"Come on, Ollie. It's me," I cry. "You know I would never hurt you."

But he sidesteps away from me.

A rush of heat squeezes my throat. If I was him, I wouldn't trust me either. "She was dying, Ollie. . . . I had to. . . . I couldn't let her suffer," I push out through gasps.

He snorts and tosses his head.

Tears surge down my cheeks and I struggle to catch my breath. "I couldn't save her."

He looks at me.

"I tried. I really did."

He moves closer.

"I'm so sorry," I choke out.

He brushes his muzzle against my cheek, and I gently take it between my hands. He doesn't fight me.

"That's a good boy. Let's get you out of here," I say, and together, we stumble through the water to the edge. But he struggles to get up the bank, his hooves slipping in the mud. I climb above him, grab a thick handful of his mane, and pull, careful not to hurt him. But his course hair slips through my muddy fingers. I tighten my grip around a section close to his withers and pull again. "Come on, boy, you can do it."

He pushes forward and I climb higher, lean back farther, and tug a little harder. Again, and again, until a final pull sends me flying back into the mud—him standing beside me, shaking and panting but safe.

I don't bother lifting myself out of the thick, wet earth. Exhausted, I lie there soaked in the loss of Strawberry.

The rain has passed, and a tiny, twinkling star in the dark sky tries to convince me that everything will be okay.

But it won't.

Now a sliver of moon is murmuring something about God having a plan.

"No! This wasn't how her life was supposed to end!" I yell, hot, angry tears pooling in my ears.

Faint tremors pulse through the ground . . . hoofbeats . . . getting stronger . . . closer. Someone's charging straight at me.

I shoot up out of the mud, hand on the gun, hoping it's Melvin.

"Josie!" I hear in the distance. It's Billie. "Josie! Josie!" she shouts again, frantically.

But there's no panic left in me. Only rage.

Shawn

It's crazy. After all these years of surviving two-ton beasts, I'm about to get taken out by some weak fool who likes to put his hands on girls. His last girlfriend ended up in the hospital same way his mom always does.

He swings the big red bolt cutters like he's going for a home run.

If I go, please let me see Mom.

A whoosh of wind. Just missed.

I'm tied to the tree. Right eye swollen shut, blood trickling from my nose and brow, lips split and stinging, and a pain on my left side I know far too well. A broken rib. And man, my wrist. They got this rope so tight I can't feel my hands. I lick the thick, salty blood dripping over my top lip and spit.

"You think you're tough, don't you?" Donny says. He's gone back to light, one-handed swings—hazy flashes of red going back and forth like he's trying to hypnotize me. The pendulum stops and a different blur of motion flies at my face. Another fist to my cheek. "Not so tough, now, are you?"

"Homie, stop playing with your food. If you're gonna knock his head off, just do it," says the tatted-face dude. He got bored after they beat me to the point where I couldn't swing back.

"I didn't sign up for this," Pete says, pacing back and forth. "Your dad told us to let the horses out and cut the fences. That's it."

"Shut up! My daddy don't run me," Donny says.

"He wouldn't even let you bring a gun. That should tell you right there he's gonna be pissed if you kill him," Pete insists.

"Did I ask you?" Donny says. "I'll kill him if I damn well please. Got plenty of space out here to bury him."

Underneath me, the muddy ground gently vibrates, and I wonder if I'm losing it. We get hurricanes in Houston, not earthquakes. The rumbling grows stronger, even stronger, and I finally recognize it. A horse—no, two—moving at full speed. *My boys*, I think, relieved.

"Really, Donny? You act like nobody knows he's out here. No way your daddy can buy this land if the police are sniffing around," Pete says.

"Forget about my daddy!" Donny screams, his voice going high. "I've waited years to catch Shawn out like this! Years!"

"All I gotta say is, I'm not digging no grave," says tatted-face.

Click-clack, bang! A shot blasting through the night.

Catches me off guard, and I flinch, ribs screaming.

"My leg, my leg! You shot me in the leg!" Donny screams.

The car's engine starts up.

"Wait for me," Pete yells, booking it toward the hole in the fence.

"That's my car!" Donny shouts, dragging himself on his elbows. "Y'all can't take my car!"

But it burns out quick.

Without the headlights, the night goes black. A saddle creaks before I hear boots hit the earth.

Then I catch something silver in the dark. A gun. Floating like a ghost. No, someone's holding it, strutting something fierce.

Josie.

Josie

Mud sucks at my boots with every step, as if the earth is trying to hold me back. But nothing can stop me from making Donny pay for what he did.

He's wriggling toward the fence on his belly like the snake he is.

"You killed my horse!" I scream before I kick his shoulder to roll him over onto his back. Trembling with rage, I point the gun down at his head.

"No, please, don't," he begs.

I stare down at his ugly, stupid face. Remembering how scared I was staring up at it alone in the alley, how helpless I felt. I'll never forget what he said.

Ain't so tough now, are you?

I drop his own words onto his face and curl my finger around the trigger, thinking about how he'll never be able to hurt anyone ever again.

Shawn

"No, Josie, don't!" I try to shout, but the pain ripping through my ribs robs my breath. I can't believe Strawberry's gone. I feel for Josie, but this won't bring her back.

"Forget that dude," Billie yells louder. She's behind the tree, taking forever to untie me.

I refuse to let Josie do this to herself. "This ain't you, Josie." I push past the fire raging up my side.

"Shawn?" she calls in my direction. "Shawn, are you okay?"

"Yeah," I lie. Good thing it's dark. The last thing she needs right now is to see me like this. "But I need you to put the gun down!"

"Donny is on our property. This is Texas. It would be self-defense," Billie assures her, still taking her sweet time with the rope.

Josie turns back toward Donny.

"Think about your kids," I urge her. "Your dream of raising them here."

"That scumbag doesn't deserve to live!" Billie shouts. "Shoot him!"

"Please, don't!" Donny says, voice high and pathetic.

"That fool ain't worth it!" I tell her.

Josie

Donny reaches for the gun.

"Don't even try it," I say, and slam my foot down onto his chest. Water squishes out of my boot and drags me right back to the creek with Strawberry.

The way she was screaming and gasping for air. Her eyes, terrified, begging for help.

I stare down at Donny—one boot pressing into his chest, the other sinking into the mud—the rest of the world fading away.

"Please, I don't want to die," he cries.

"Shut up!" I yell, hard, shaky breath hissing through my teeth. I want him to suffer like Strawberry did. I want him to feel the panic, the confusion, the terror . . . the excruciating pain . . . the awful stillness that never ends.

"Please. I beg you!"

I drill my eyes into his.

"For the love of God!"

I swallow the prayer whole. It's too much, and I look away. But the words are still in me, reminding me who I am.

When I look back down, all I see is a small, broken soul.

I take my boot off Donny's chest, yank my other one out of the mud, and lower the gun.

Shawn

Mud like skin where my mouth and nose used to be. *I can't breathe . . . I can't breathe.* The moon swings, pounding my jaw. It kicks me in the ribs and I hit the ground. I get up. Fight back, but my arms are soggy green beans. The trees don't even try to help. They all have their phones out, filming. The phones spread their wings, claws outstretched, and head straight for my face before—*pow!*—a shot rings out.

"Huhhh!" I gasp, heart pounding, aching eyes barely opening to the blinding florescent lights overhead.

"Shawn!" Josie rushes to the side of my hospital bed.

Her eyes are puffy, like she's been crying. Outside the window behind her, the sky is dark. "You okay?" she asks.

Now I am, I think, letting out a deep breath. "Yeah," I say, throat scratchy and dry.

She presses the button to sit me up a little straighter and grabs a cup off the side table beside my unfinished dinner. "Here, have some water," she says, bringing the straw to my lips.

I try to sit up even more on my own, but it's like a boot being slammed into my ribs all over again. "Ugh," I groan, and ease back.

"Relax, you're going to hurt yourself."

"You don't even know, Josie," I say, my mind going back to those bolt cutters just missing my head. "I was a dead man. You saved me."

Josie

"I didn't save anybody," I say, wishing I could wave a magic wand over Shawn's swollen, black eyes . . . over his broken nose and busted lip . . . over the bruises traveling from his cheek, down his neck, and disappearing under his hospital gown . . . over his struggling breath . . . his fractured rib . . . his wrapped wrist. And make it all go away. Wishing I could bring Strawberry back.

"Nah, trust . . . you did."

"How can you say that? You're messed up in the hospital and it's all my fault."

"This ain't on you, Josie."

"But none of this would've happened if you hadn't come to help. I'm the one who dragged you into this."

"What are you talking about? You weren't even there. It was Billie who got me into that fight. But at the end of the day, Donny did this. Dude was trying to kill me."

I gently touch his bruised cheek.

He takes my hand and holds it to his chest. "But I'm here because you saved me. For real, it was about to be lights out. And you rode in like my very own hero."

"Heroes don't kill their horses or leave their boyfriends bleeding to death." I squeeze my eyes shut and start crying all over again.

"Come on, Josie. Don't do that to yourself. It was dark. You had no idea what kind of shape I was in. And I know what happened with Strawberry wasn't easy. But you had the courage to do the hard thing, and now she's free."

I imagine Strawberry's spirit running in the back pasture, wind blowing through her mane. "Papa believes that when you die, you become a part of everything. I guess there's nothing freer than that."

"Except that we're already one with everything now . . . already free," Shawn says.

Sounds nice but I'm too tired to think about what it really means.

"At least that's what my mom taught me. If only people realized most cages were made of thoughts."

"Here you go getting all deep again."

He chuckles. "I told you I can take it there . . . laid up in the hospital or not."

His phone buzzes.

"Want me to get it?" I ask.

His smile is gone. "Nah, it's probably just Sterling again."

"Yeah, he's been blowing my parents' phones up all day too."

"I bet. Wants to act like he's all sorry now that he almost got me killed."

I don't know what to say. What kind of parent does that? Makes me feel ridiculous for complaining about Mom. She might be overbearing and a little too bougie for her own good, but she'd never intentionally try to hurt me or put me in any kind of danger.

"Way too late for apologies," Shawn continues, bloodshot eyes so full of hurt I can barely keep from crying again myself.

I lean down to gently kiss his lips.

His lifts his head a bit like he wants more.

I brush my lips across his wet cheeks and take my kisses slowly around his face.

"Oh, Josie. You don't even know," he says.

One more kiss on his lips before I whisper, "My parents said I can stay the night with you."

His swollen face spreads with a smile. "Word?"

"Yeah, they don't think you should be alone."

"Good, because I don't want to be alone."

"Guess they're not worried about us messing around with the condition you're in."

His smile grows wider. "I love it when people underestimate me."

Shawn

After the night nurse asks me all these random questions in her singsong voice and leaves, Josie carefully climbs into bed with me. Tucks herself against my good side. We should have another three hours before the nurse comes in to check on me again.

We flip through the channels on the TV mounted to the wall and settle on a show called *Friends*. A few of the characters are familiar from memes. Should definitely be better than *Law & Order* or *Cops*.

But it's not. Two episodes in and Josie is pissed at this Ross dude for cheating on this Rachel girl, even though she'd broken up with him. One minute, Josie's fussing at the screen, "It was a break, not a breakup." And the next minute, she's looking up at me. "I know this isn't the best time, and I feel awful for bringing it up right now, but it's literally driving me crazy. So I have to know: What's up with Tara?"

"Nothing," I answer, mad at Ross for bringing me into this.

She takes her hand off my chest. "So you didn't sleep with her?"

"Nah, I wouldn't do that."

"You mean to tell me you've never slept with her?"

My bruised insides flare with panic, but I come clean. “Once or twice, but it was years ago.”

She rises onto her elbow, face scrunched up. “Once or twice? What? Did you forget?”

“No, no . . . one of the times, she just . . . well, you know—”

“Ugh, of course!”

“But it’s not like that anymore.”

Josie

Shawn has already been through enough. *I know . . . I know.* But all I can think about is that picture of him and Tara on the Ferris wheel . . . her finding a million little ways to touch him the night we met . . . the embroidered cherries on the backs of her jean pockets as she rushed off to meet her boyfriend. I hate myself for remembering that! I can just imagine Shawn sliding his hand into one of her cherry-covered pockets. *Gross!*

"When?" I ask.

"Like three years ago?"

"Before or after you met me?"

"Does it matter?"

"Yes, gives me context."

"After."

"How soon after."

He sighs. "I don't know. Maybe a month."

"So you met me and then slept with her?"

"You left without even giving me your number, remember?"

"But how could you even date a girl like that? She's clearly a . . . a . . ." I want to say *ho*, but all the programming drilled into my head about it being a regressive, slut-shaming term that reinforces double standards stops me.

But what if it applies to boys and girls? What if I missed the meeting when all the girls of the world decided that since boys were hos, they wanted to be hos too. Like, if you can't beat them, join them, huh? Um, no! How about boys need to stop being hos too! "A ho."

"Damn," he says, "that's harsh. You don't even know her like that."

"So she hasn't slept with a ton of guys?"

"Yeah, but she has issues," he says, defending her. "Why are we talking about her again?

"Okay, so let's talk about you. Do you like to sleep around too?"

"Nah, not at all."

The way he's staying so chill is starting to make me feel awful. I should be taking care of him, not grilling him. I have questions, yes, but there's no need for the hostility. "So how did you end up messing around with her?" I ask, softening my tone.

"I've known her since I first hit the junior circuit . . . almost ten years. We were kids back then. She was there for me when I was missing my mom. And then I was there for her when her mom had an affair. We were just friends for the longest. And when we got older . . . I don't know . . . I was lonely I guess, and she was . . . there. But nothing happened last week, I swear. Not a kiss . . . nothing. As you know, I was going through a lot and you . . . you . . ."

"Weren't there," I admit, hating myself for blocking him. When Shawn told me what his dad had said about his real dad being married and wanting nothing to do with him, it literally made me nauseous.

"But none of that matters anymore. Can we please just forget about everything else and focus on us?" he asks, reaching across his body to take my hand.

I meet him halfway, slide my fingers between his, and our hands rest together on his chest. "But what if we get into another fight and I'm not there again?"

"I mean, hopefully you'll never ghost me like that without at least hearing me out," he says, eyes locked on mine like he's searching for some kind of reassurance.

"I won't."

"Nah, for real? Because that . . . that was rough."

"I promise," I tell him. "But you have to promise to never keep anything from me. No more secrets."

"I can do that."

"And know that if we ever do go on a break, you better not act up," I say, half joking.

He laughs but then gets serious. "Nah, we're not doing that."

"Doing what?"

"Breaks."

"No breaks?"

"Nah."

"Like ever?"

He pulls my palm in close with his fingers, eyes on mine. "You're it for me, Josie, like straight up."

My heart flies open. "You too."

Shawn

Man, I wish I wasn't hurt. I want to sit up and kiss her so bad.

Josie must notice because she leans over to give me her lips again. So soft and warm and gentle I can't help but moan.

She pulls away. "You okay?"

"Yeah, I'm straight."

"Good," she says, looking at me the same way she always has.

How? I wonder. I nearly made myself jump when I finally made it to the bathroom and caught a glimpse of myself. I'm a monster. And here she is gazing into my eyes like I'm the most beautiful man in the world.

"What?"

"I'm so blessed to have you."

"I'm the one who's blessed," she says, and softly strokes my face.

I can spend all night like this. The rest of my life like this.

She brushes her lips across mine and kisses me again.

I can't believe that this girl is mine. And that I'm hers. And that she could see herself being my family one day. Bringing life into this world. It almost feels like some type of miracle. "I love you, Josie."

Josie

His words cover my body, attach to my skin, and sink into me. Fill me. First with relief and then with something beyond happiness. It's the best feeling in the entire world . . . so pure and sweet. "I love you too," I say.

He smiles the cutest smile.

And I reach for his lips again. *Careful, careful* . . . I have to watch myself.

He lets out a sound that sends pulses deep down inside me.

And I forget all about being gentle.

"Ngh." He grimaces.

"Oh my gosh. I'm so sorry."

"I'm good," he says.

But his face tells a different story.

"The nurse said you could push that button for pain if you needed to," I remind him.

"That button," he says, and laughs under his breath, "that button will do you in if you let it. I've seen riders lose everything to painkillers."

"I never thought about that," I admit. "With all the injuries y'all get, they must be handing them out like candy."

"Exactly. They had my dad messed up for a while when

I was young. Good thing he was strong enough to kick 'em, but they were no joke."

"Damn," I say, surprised by the admiration in his voice. His relationship with his dad is something I don't fully understand. But clearly, there's still a lot of love there.

"So yeah, I'd rather deal with the pain. At least I know that's temporary."

I love how strong Shawn is. Makes me feel safe with him. "Well, I guess we'll have to go easy on all the kissing for now."

He laughs a little. "Unfortunately."

"I hate that my parents were right," I say, laying my head back down beside his.

"Give me a day or two and I'll be good to go."

I laugh. "Boy, shut up."

"I'm serious, though."

I grab the remote from the dip in the blanket between his calves. "Let's watch something else."

Shawn

I unwrap the bandage from around my ribs. Slowly slip a white tee over my head. It's still dark outside my window, but rest time is over. The Championship is Sunday, which means I only have six days to prepare.

Half my life, I've been risking my neck on the backs of bulls, afraid it was the only way to keep Sterling's love. But a love like that is not worth having. Can't believe it took me so long to realize.

Whatever, though, gotta keep it moving. I'm about to switch things up and put my energy into horses. But before I do, I need one last ride to go out on top. Say goodbye to the sport and my fans at the largest rodeo in the world, Rodeo-Houston, right here in my hometown.

Josie doesn't want to hear any of it. *But you can't!* she must've cried a million times yesterday. After I got discharged from the hospital, she drove me home and took care of me until her curfew. Ice packs, chicken soup, chocolate, ice cream, and gentle kisses. She even tried to convince her parents to let her stay over to keep nursing me. But they weren't having it, especially on a school night.

Thank God.

Don't get me wrong, I love Josie. Nah, I can't even lie, I *need* Josie. But being all cozy and lovey-dovey is not the move for me right now. It was nice while it lasted, crucial even, but it's time to focus.

I grab my hat off the hook by the front door and head out to the practice facility. Not that I plan to get onto the backs of any bulls today. I'm not crazy. I just need to let my body know what's coming.

I'm not even out of the neighborhood, and it's already grumbling that it would rather be on the sofa, snuggled up with Josie. Man, who knew driving took so much abdominal work? Even though I'm steering with my left hand, my ribs are killing me.

After the shape Donny and his crew left me in, I'm sure Melvin is betting his entire bankroll against me. Word on the street is that he's still collecting wagers. Little does he know, I'm about to get this W and kill all his plans. Not that Mimi and Papa would ever sell to that scumbag now, but I know he's gotta have another property lined up to clean his dirty cash.

Actually, Mimi and Papa aren't selling to anyone. Josie said they were pumped about her proposal to keep the land in the family. On the sofa last night, she read it to me from her phone, beaming with pride. And I could see why—restaurant, music, campfires, s'mores, trail rides, weddings, events—it's gonna be sick.

In the parking lot, I push open the door to my truck and step out, tiny knives stabbing me in the side as I take in the familiar smell of manure and wet earth . . . the familiar sight of the sun peeking over the tree line. I turn to face the ring. Might be run-down and rusty as hell, but this place took me from being a scared, broken little boy to a strong man.

So many days, I worked from sunup till sundown, Sterling in my ear: *Stay ahead of him! Don't lean into the spin! Squeeze and lift. Now, lock yourself in!* And when I wanted to quit: *Come on, you've got this! Doesn't matter if you get bucked, most important thing is that you get back up.*

I still haven't read his texts. He's been sending message after message since he found out what happened. Can't imagine what he has to say for himself.

Walking past the ring, I watch a couple ranch hands, ankle deep in mud, wrangling a beginner bull through the narrow alleys. I head toward the wooden bleachers on the other side, my hat pulled down low. People around here are used to seeing dudes beat up, whether by bulls or bar fights, but my face is something special.

When I climb the stands, each step pulls at my ribs, reminding me that my body is even more busted than my face. After only a few rows, I sit down, wondering how the hell I'm about to pull this off. Bull riding is already the most dangerous sport in the world, but it gets ten times more dangerous when you're riding injured.

One wrong move could get me killed.

A rank bull slams the gate and then stares me down, as if to ask, *You coming to ride me or what?*

"Not today, Stitches," I say, imagining being on his back tomorrow. Not to ride, just to sit in the chute with his weight beneath me. Feel things out.

Should I do the same thing the next day? Or should I try to stand on the balance ball for an hour? Or maybe get on the bucking barrel to reignite that muscle memory? Too much? Not enough? But I don't have much time. I need to start training, but how?

I'm not sure what pain I should listen to and what I should ignore. How far can I push myself without making my injuries worse? I've always had Sterling watching my every move, helping me figure that all out.

Man, who am I fooling? Sterling might not be my dad anymore, but if I want to ride on Sunday, I still need him as my trainer. I'm not trying to take an L, or worse, get myself killed.

This is strictly business.

Six days. And after I win and give him his cut of the prize money, I won't have to see him or talk to him again.

I pull out my phone.

Josie

"Where's Daddy?" I ask, walking into the kitchen.

Mom's sitting at the breakfast table in her robe with a plate of sliced boiled egg, cheese, and grape tomatoes. *A deconstructed omelet*, as she likes to call it. "Good morning to you too."

"Oh, sorry. . . . Morning."

"Your dad is in his office prepping for that big meeting with the bankers. So it's probably best that you don't bother him," she says, and takes a sip of her coffee.

"Wait, about financing for the ranch?" I ask, and excitedly grab a tomato from the plate waiting for me on the island and pop it in my mouth.

"Yep," she says matter-of-factly.

Part of me feels like I've won, like I've finally beat her. But a different part can't celebrate when she's not fully on board. As much as I try not to, I still care what Mom thinks. I carry my plate to the breakfast table and slide onto the bench across from her. "You didn't like the proposal?"

"No, it was good. Really good, actually," she says, as if she's surprised. "Your dad had to expand on it, but he's using all your ideas in the meeting today."

"Thanks," I reply, heart swelling with pride. But then I wonder. "Well, why don't you seem happy about it, then?"

"Oh, I'm fine," she says with a quick wave of her hand. "It's not the vision I had for the ranch restaurant or where I thought we'd be investing most of our money for the next five years. But the numbers make sense in the long term. So I'll have to adjust."

The numbers? How can you be so detached? This is your family's land too! I want to shout, but ask, "Don't you miss life on the ranch?"

"Not really," she says, bringing a triangle of cheese to her mouth.

A picture from Mimi's album pops into my head. Mom in pigtails atop a brown mare whose tail was braided the same way. "Not even a little bit?"

"I can't say that I do."

"Why?" I ask. It's hard to imagine growing up somewhere so beautiful and not wanting to go back whenever you could.

"You want to know what I was doing at your age before school?"

I stare at the freckles tracing her cheekbones. "What?"

"Mucking stalls."

"Before school? What about breakfast?"

"Oh, I helped with that too."

"Seriously? What time did you get up?"

"Let me see . . . school mornings . . . five o'clock. Weekends . . . seven. And summer . . . six."

"What?" I say in disbelief. And here I was thinking I had it bad every time Mimi woke me up before nine.

"Yeah, there was a lot of work to do, and we had to get it

done before the heat hit. Me and your uncle Jimmy. Trust me, one time dragging that pasture under the scorching sun, and you'd be begging to get up at the crack of dawn."

"What about Mr. George and the ranch hands?"

"Your grandparents didn't hire them until after I graduated."

"Why?"

"Money, Josie! It doesn't grow on trees!"

Even though I should be used to it by now, the way she suddenly flips and gets all harsh feels like a shock to my system, and I tear up.

"I'm sorry I snapped. . . . It's not your fault," she says, lowering her voice. "I'm glad we've been able to give you such a good life. I really am. And it's great that you've been able to enjoy the ranch with your grandparents. It is. But my experience growing up there was hard. Grueling really.

"Which is why I escaped the first chance I got. Your Uncle Jimmy too. He . . ." Her voice breaks. "He hated horses. When we were little, one bit his arm and after that, he wanted nothing to do with them. He was so desperate to get away from the ranch after I left that he ran off to the military and got himself killed."

I watch as tears roll down Mom's face, realizing the only other time I've seen her cry was at Uncle Jimmy's funeral. Seeing her puffy, red face when she'd stepped out of the limo was as bad as Billie wailing or the heartbreaking song coming from that weird trumpet or watching his casket, draped with the American flag, being lowered into the ground.

Awful.

She lets out a deep breath. "So yeah, that's why I'm not as excited as you," she says, and wipes her face. "But like I said, I'll get over it."

"I'm really sorry, Mom," I say, feeling like my words aren't enough. I get up and go sit beside her. Give her a hug.

She wraps her arms around me, smelling like roses and vanilla and fresh rain. So cozy and warm and sweet. Pretty much how my whole life has been.

"I know I've had it good," I say into her shoulder, "and I can act spoiled sometimes."

She lets go of me. "That's not your fault either," she says, taking my hands in hers. "It's funny. Your dad and I have been so hell-bent on shielding you from the struggles of our childhoods that we've likely made yours too easy. Let me tell you: life is not easy for anybody. If growing up on the ranch with your grandparents taught me one thing, it's how to work hard."

"Maybe you and Dad didn't make me do as much work as Mimi and Papa," I say, "but it's not like I'm completely incapable, you know."

"As much? You don't do anything around here," she says with a smile.

"I keep my room clean."

She gives me a look.

"Well, most of the time."

She doesn't change her playful side-eye.

"Okay, I keep my room clean at the ranch. Here, I don't . . . it's hard when I know I'm not really expected to," I admit.

"Goodness, looking back on it now, thank God we were busy, and you had to spend so much time at the ranch. I can't imagine how spoiled you'd be if you didn't have *any* chores or responsibilities. You'd be insufferable."

I laugh. "Gee, Mom, thanks."

She laughs with me. "I'm serious."

"I guess that means you approve of me working at the ranch after graduation."

"I don't think you even know what you've signed up for. You're going to be wishing you were hanging out in New York with Brittney and Sage." She laughs. "The ranch has more help these days, but bringing this plan of yours to fruition is still going to be a ton of work."

"You're wrong," I tell her, straight-faced. "I was never into New York like that. It's not that I don't think it's cool, but it's also cold and dirty and nobody even speaks to each other on the street. You and Daddy met there, and that's nice. But it's not my thing. Y'all have taken me everywhere . . . literally shown me the world. And after seeing it, I know in my heart of hearts that the ranch is the only place I want to be."

"Okay, sorry," she says, looking totally sincere.

Then it hits me: maybe she hasn't taken me seriously all these years because I never did much to earn her respect. "And the hard work will be good for me," I continue. "I'm pumped."

"You're right, it will," she agrees. "And honestly, the ranch will be good for me too. I've been holding on to my grudge for far too long. Longer than it was healthy for me.

And really, it's not fair. Your grandparents were doing the best they could. And it was Jimmy's decision to go fight in a war. Not theirs or anybody else's."

"So does that mean you're going to start riding and shooting and fishing with us?" I ask, trying not to get sad about Strawberry.

"Yeah, no more missing out on all the good stuff. It's time to move on," she says, and looks at her skinny gold watch. "Goodness, it's time for you to get your butt to school!"

I glance at the clock on the oven: 7:35 a.m. "Oh my gosh! I'm gonna be so late," I say before taking a sip of her coffee, stealing a slice of her cheese, and rushing out.

"Thief!" she shouts playfully.

"You snooze, you lose! See, you and Daddy taught me more than you thought."

Shawn

"Already?" Josie asks. "But we haven't even been on the phone twenty minutes."

"I know, but I'm about to hop in my ice bath and then I still have to do my breathing exercises before bed," I explain.

"It's only six o'clock."

I dump another bag of ice into the running water. "Yeah, Sterling wants me asleep by seven."

"I still don't get how you were with him all day and didn't discuss anything."

"We talked about plenty. Mapped out a whole plan for the week."

"But what about everything he said in his messages?"

"Nah, I'm not trying to deal with all that now." I'd finally read through Sterling's messages. Turns out, Mom didn't know my real father was married. He had a house here but traveled back and forth to Dallas for business. They dated for two years and even talked about getting married—that is, until she got pregnant with me.

The crazy part? He did die from a stroke, but not before I was born. A year after Mom passed. Sterling saw it on Facebook.

"But aren't you curious about your siblings?" she asks.

"That's just not what I'm focused on right now," I tell her. I have a finite amount of energy. And all of it needs to go toward those eight seconds on Sunday.

"I just can't believe he didn't bring any of it up today."

The water starts gurgling and I shut it off. "Yeah, he kept it professional like I asked."

"Humph," she says, as if finally ready to drop it.

"Well, my bath is ready so I should probably go."

"Two more minutes?"

"I'm supposed to be using this time to visualize my ride. It's a whole thing."

"Please. Going back to school today was a lot. Explaining everything to my friends felt like living through the nightmare all over again."

"Oh, dang. I'm sorry. You want to talk about it?"

"No, I just want to keep you a few more minutes."

"Okay, hold on," I say, moving the phone from the sink, where I have it on speaker, to the edge of the tub. I slip off my clothes and step in. "Nnngh," I grunt, and clench my teeth as I slowly lower myself into the freezing water. Brutal. But I know it's what my body needs.

"You all right over there?"

"Yeah, I'm straight."

"I miss you," she says in the sweetest voice.

I close my eyes and imagine her pretty face, her perfect lips. Off task but it feels so much better than the cold clawing at me. "I miss you too."

"Are you sure I can't come see you after school tomorrow?"

"Yeah, I'm sure."

"Not even for like ten minutes?"

"Sorry. It's not like I don't want to see you too, but I only have six days. Not even because today is gone. So that's five. Time for me to lock all the way in."

"You act like one little kiss and hug is going to kill you?"

"It could."

"Don't say that. It'll make me more worried than I already am."

"It's true, though," I say, staring at the huge scar on my thigh from when I got gored by a bull at fourteen. Just missed my femoral artery. "Bull riders die all the time. And as you know, I'm not exactly a hundred percent."

"So why are you doing this, then?"

"I told you . . . one last ride to go out on top. Plus, I need to make sure it's game over for Melvin."

"But you literally just got out of the hospital. How are you even going to ride with a fractured rib and sprained wrist?"

"It's just what I have to deal with," I say, freezing claws fading as the numbness sets in. "Comes with the territory."

"But you don't *have* to."

"Yeah, I do."

"Do you really, though?"

"Yeah, I gotta try."

"But you've already won the world finals. What's another win? And who cares about Melvin? My grandparents aren't even selling the ranch anymore."

"Look, Josie," I say, trying to stay patient, "it's not just about the title and the cash. You have to understand, I've spent the last decade of my life training to be number one. It doesn't matter that I won the PBR last year. The grind to the top starts over at every rodeo.

"And now we're talking about the biggest rodeo in the world, in my *hometown*. I've already made it through three rounds, and I only have one ride left. I'm not about to just give that up.

"And I'm not about to forget Melvin either." I keep trying to explain. "He needs to pay for what he did. I'm about to hit him where it hurts. One blow and he'll be too far under to get back up. It's about time for somebody to shut that man down for good."

"But why does it have to be you?" she asks.

And after all of that, we're back at square one. "Look, Josie, I love you. I really do. And I promise that after Sunday we can hang out and talk as much as you want. But right now I gotta go."

Josie

"Ladies and gentlemen, and last but not least, we've got Shawn Williams, right here from Houston, Texas!" the announcer says over the loudspeaker.

"Look, it's Shawn! It's Shawn!" Kiana says, pointing to the Jumbotron. She and her sister are standing at the railing, holding up their signs—"Ride Tough, Cowboy!" and "We Love You, Shawn!" scrawled in letters as colorful as the barrettes at the ends of their ponytails.

His helmet does a good job hiding his bruises and cuts, but I can still see them. I take a deep breath, fighting the fear of losing him.

"At just eighteen, Shawn became the youngest PBR World Champion in history," the announcer continues. "And tonight, he'll be making another big mark on the sport by retiring. That's right, folks, this will be Shawn's final ride! Y'all might want to hold on to your hats for this showdown because he's about to square off with none other than the baddest bull in the business—Hellfire! They've got history, and it ain't pretty!"

Eyes wide, I whip my head toward Shelly in the seat beside me, searching for something, anything, that might help me relax. What are the chances of Shawn drawing Hellfire not once but twice in his short professional career?

She tucks her freshly silk-pressed hair behind her ear and looks over at me, eyes calm as ever.

How? I wonder, before I remember this is not her first rodeo.

"Oh, Shawn didn't tell you he drew Hellfire?"

I swallow hard and shake my head. No, Shawn didn't tell me. The only message he sent me today was a plain *Thanks* in response to my super-long, love-drenched good-luck message. In fact, I've barely talked to him this week. Ten-minute conversations before his evening ice bath, that's it.

I follow her eyes up to the giant screen.

HELLFIRE

Owner/Stock Contractor: Rex Brown/Canyon Ranch

Rank: #1 in the World

Average Bull Score: 47.5

Buck-Off Percentage: 97.55%

Average Buck-Off Time: 1.88 Seconds

Specialty: Explosive Strength, High Jumps, Unpredictable Spins

"Don't worry, sweetie," she says, gentle eyes back on me. "Sterling has had Shawn riding that bull in his mind for hours already. And really, pulling Hellfire is the best thing that could've happened. The higher the rank, the higher the score."

"That's right!" Trey shouts from the other side of me. "No risk, no reward!"

"That's my boy right there! Let's go!" Rob adds from beside him.

Are y'all insane? I want to scream. This is the same bull who nearly killed Shawn. Who literally has a reputation for going for blood. I swear I wish Billie was here. She would agree with me. But she doesn't trust herself to be in the same building as Melvin or Donny, who's already out on bail.

Shelly goes quiet and looks back up at the screen, which is now showing Shawn in the chute. She reaches for the small silver cross hanging from her neck, presses it between her fingers, and closes her eyes.

I'm too scared to close my eyes. But Papa taught me that there's always a portal open between me and God. *Please bring my love back to me safe and sound.*

Shawn

Sometimes you can prepare all you want. Sacrifice. Stay disciplined. Dial all the way in. And still not be ready for the nightmare you face.

Mine is beneath me, even bigger than the last time I rode him. Muscles rippling, snorting, back legs twitching, body banging against the steel bars—like he can't wait to bust out and finish what he started.

"Tighten it again," I tell Sterling, the pounding in my chest, ears, and head way louder than the crowd.

Standing on the rails of the chute, he leans over and yanks on the bull rope.

The handle bites into my glove, but I still say, "Tighter," trying to feel something besides this fear.

"You gotta stay loose!"

"Okay," I say, and try channeling the energy into balancing my weight. Into what I can control. Gotta get these nerves in check before I take my wrap.

"That's right, focus on your seat. And remember to keep your hand low."

Solid advice but it's hard to focus on anything with the memory of my last ride on Hellfire banging on every door inside me.

Sterling must sense I'm having trouble because he leans

in. "You've had the grit to get this far. . . . Don't let that go! Hellfire ain't no worse than the beasts you've been facing your whole life! Time to dig in and ride him out!"

His pep talk cuts through the noise, and I shift in the seat, finding my center.

Sterling leans in even more, his head nearly touching my helmet, and locks his eyes on mine. "You've got this, son!"

Son.

A word I thought I never wanted to hear from him again now feels like a strong hand, dragging me outside to face my fear.

I was in bed, lights out, the first time he called me son. He barged into my room, opened my window, and told me to get up. The light and cold felt like a shock to my system, but I didn't move. Wasn't his first attempt to get me out of my room since the accident.

But this time, after words didn't work, he pulled my covers off. It had been three weeks. Guess he was like enough is enough.

I protested and yanked them back up to my chin.

A tug of war ensued.

I lost. Foul smells, crumbs, chip bags, and *The Adventures of Nat Love* in the air. I buried my face into my knees and cried.

He cried too, right beside me, sitting on the edge of my bed. Then after a while, he said, "It's me and you now, son."

Three hours later, I was sitting on the back of my first baby bull. Terrifying, but after I made eight seconds, I knew I could do anything.

I lean forward, tighten my thighs against Hellfire's sides, take my wrap, and let out a long breath, finally ready to put this nightmare to rest.

Give the nod.

Josie

The red, brockle-faced bull blasts out of the gate, Shawn's free hand shoots up in the air, and I forget how to breathe.

Shawn

A quick, sharp spin. Howling from my ribs and wrist. But my heart is louder. *You move, I move!* and I keep my weight over his shoulders. Stay with him.

Josie

Hind legs straight up in the air and, oh my gosh, my heart is free-falling.

Shawn

Dropping and it's do or die. *Don't quit! Don't quit! Don't quit!* and I take the hit, whole body screaming. Down and around and the tip of his horn is two inches from my face.

Josie

I lurch forward in my seat, praying the horn doesn't hit. *Thank God*, I think, grabbing Shelly's arm. But the pain on his face still makes me feel sick.

Shawn

My stomach in my throat as we go near vertical again. And now a twist that rips us back down! *Nah, bruh*, I think. I didn't come this far for nothing.

Josie

Seven . . . almost there.

Shawn

The buzzer blares, and it's *the best sound.*

I slide off, hit the ground hard, and the bullfighter steps in. Now I'm up, throwing my arms in the air. Arena going crazy.

Man, I just made the whistle on Hellfire . . . Hellfire! I can't even begin to describe how this feels. Like magic . . . no, better than magic because I did this! Gave it everything I had, and all my work . . . all my pain . . . paid off.

Thank God!

"Holy cow! A massive ninety-three points!" the announcer says over the loudspeaker. "There it is, folks. Give it up for your new RodeoHouston bull-riding champion!"

"What!" I yell, and without thinking I'm running toward the man standing on the chute with his arms in the air. He might be messed up right now, but that doesn't take away from the fact that he's the one who taught me how to hold on when the ride gets rough. The one who taught me I could be as tough as I believed I was. Taught me that I could do anything if I tried hard enough.

The one who stepped up and made sure I didn't have to grow up without a father. I didn't have to ride to earn his love. Nah, riding was simply the best way he knew how to show me love. I see that now. He knew it would either make me or break me after the accident. And he bet on make me.

A gamble that paid off big.

His arms are around me. "I'm so proud of you, son."

And it's like all his apologies that I refused to allow myself to feel are finally sinking in. He might not be blood, but he's family. "Thanks, Dad."

Josie

"What a moment," the announcer says as the whole arena watches Shawn give his dad a long hug on the Jumbotron. "We're witnessing two generations of riders tonight. One who set the stage and the other who just claimed the crown. Nothing says rodeo like family!"

I'm in tears. Shelly's in tears. Rob is in tears. Trey is trying to play it off, but I just saw a tear slip down his cheek too. The girls are already bored and begging for cotton candy.

I can't believe Shawn just won RodeoHouston! Honestly, it seemed impossible. But he did it.

Thank God he didn't listen to me when I tried to discourage him.

Thank God he didn't let me come over after school.

Thank God he wouldn't text me when he woke up in the morning.

Or from the practice facility.

Or after he got into bed.

Shawn waves to the crowd, and now he's blowing me kiss after kiss after kiss.

I send them flying right back, my body brimming with admiration for his will and determination. "That's my man right there!"

Shawn

Dang, I think, staring at the wildflowers and string lights lining the gravel path to the old barn, the sheer curtains swaying in its doorway, *my girl has been putting in work.*

Walking up with Lil Love, I can hear her hammering over a Cleo Sol song.

I tie his reins to the hitching post and head inside. "Yo, Josie!"

But she's in her own world, back to me, arm raised mid-swing, singing.

We need your heart
We need your soul
We need your strength through this cold world.

She's been working on turning this barn into a showroom every moment she's had since my final ride a few weeks ago. She's barely had time to hang. Her vision sounded cool over the phone but, man, seeing it in person is a whole different thing. Up high, four wheels from her great-great-grandparents' old wagon, wrapped in greenery and lights, hang from the rafters. On the floor, waiting, are bathroom doors: one decorated with Uncle Jimmy's encased military jacket and the other her great-grandmother's lace dress. On the walls, her ancestors look into the room from photos in thick, ornate frames. It's almost as if you can feel their presence, blessing the place.

I sneak up on Josie from behind and grab her waist.

Makes her jump. "Boy!" she says, turning around.

I kiss her. "I see you've been working your magic in here."

"I'm no designer, but I'm doing my best."

"Could've fooled me!"

Makes her laugh. "Honestly, I didn't even know I had it in me. I suppose I've helped my mom with projects before, but getting to do this in my own style is different. I've kind of been obsessed."

"I can tell."

"Not that I'm ever going to stop training horses. But right now, getting funding is everything. I just hope this is good enough—"

"Are you kidding me? Those investors would be out of their minds not to back this place," I say, scanning the room. "Look at the way you pay tribute to your ancestors. And it's not just your family's history you're showcasing . . . it's American history. The kind a lot of people don't know. So the fact that everybody who rolls up to Riley Ranch will be taking it all in? Man, what! It's so good."

"Well, thank you," she says, beaming.

"You're very welcome."

She tosses the hammer, and now her hand is around my neck as she kisses me—soft at first, then commanding. We kiss through the entire song.

I pull away. "Mimi's gonna let me have it if I don't bring you back soon. She's almost done with dinner."

"What's she cooking?"

"Meat loaf and cheesy potatoes."

"Papa's favorite," she says, smiling as if I'd just said fried fish and hush puppies.

"No wonder why he looked so happy tuning up his banjo."

"Oh, he's already got the banjo out?" she says, doing the cutest little dance. "I'm ready!"

I stare at her, thinking about how perfect she is. *Never could I have imagined. Not in my wildest dreams.*

"Oh, wait, before we go, help me get this up."

I follow her eyes down to a huge frame, leaning against the wall. I step back to look at it. The photo is of a young girl standing in front of the river with a horse. She's covered in mud and has a huge smile on her face. "Is that you and Strawberry?"

"No, it's my great-grandmother Barbara and her horse Pearl."

"Wow, the resemblance is crazy," I say, and wrap my arm around her.

Josie leans into me. "I know, right. When it came back from the framer this morning, I must've sat down in front of it for almost an hour. Obviously, I'd seen the photo before. But looking at it blown up like this? I don't know . . . it felt like I was there . . . inside it."

I pull her closer.

"At first I was pissed," she continues. "I was cursing at

the river and all. Things got dark. I must've cried for twenty minutes. Then I just kind of sat there until . . . you know how fireflies blink on and off and on and off over the grass at night?"

"Yeah."

"Well, it was like that. Then the light inside me just kind of stayed on. And before I knew it, all I could feel was love. I swear I was glowing with it. And it was all around me, everywhere, in everything."

"Dang, that sounds incredible."

"Yeah, it made me think about what you were saying in the hospital about being one with everything now . . . like, not waiting until we die. I just wanted the feeling to last forever, you know?"

"He's the same yesterday and today and forever," I say, repeating something Shelly always says.

"Who?" Josie asks, stepping back.

"God," I answer, and lift the frame. But it's heavy and I can't see around it.

Josie helps guide it onto the hook. "You mean *She's* the same yesterday and today and forever?"

I laugh and make sure the frame is steady before I let go. "He? She? Like you said, it's all Love."

Josie

Outside, the sun is lowering into the trees, turning everything golden blue.

"Are we really doing this?" I ask Shawn.

"Do you want to?" he asks, and swings up onto Lil Love.

"I do."

"Come on, then," he says, reaching down.

I take his hand and pull myself up to face him.

He passes one of the reins over my head. "You good?"

I nod, still iffy about the idea of riding backward. *I can't see where we're going. What if we hit a dip and Lil Love gets spooked? This is only his second time at the ranch.*

"Don't worry. Hold on."

I grip Shawn's thighs, and we start down the gravel path, slow and easy, my body relaxing with every step. And by the time we reach the field, I've forgotten all about myself.

Black, outstretched wings wobble high in the sky. A dragonfly flits past. Unseen birds chirp and caw and screech from green crowns all around. The wind shivers in the trees. Oh, and the wildflowers! The field is littered with blooms: patches of yellow, pink, orange, and blue. The ridiculous goodness of it all makes me throw my head back and laugh.

"What?" Shawn asks.

"It's gorgeous out here."

"Yeah, like a dream."

"I'm so used to it that I keep forgetting to notice."

"Can't do that."

We go back to riding in silence. And, again, I find myself wanting this feeling of oneness to last forever. *Possible?* I don't have the answer.

All I know is that in this moment, I'm here, with Shawn. I stare at his beautiful face, still faintly bruised on his right cheek.

His eyes meet mine, and I swear the whole sky leans in to tell me a secret: *heaven is now.*

Acknowledgments

This book wouldn't exist without my early memories of going to RodeoHouston. Thanks, Mommy and Daddy! The way you raised me—to never give up and to hold tight to God's love—is still how I ride through life.

Big thanks to RodeoHouston for the sights, smells, and flavors that inspired these pages . . . and for giving me a reason to break out my boots, hats, and bolo ties every spring.

I am deeply grateful to the many books that are helping to reclaim the long-overlooked legacy of African Americans in rodeo and cowboy history. In addition to teaching me about legendary figures like Nat Love, Mathew Hooks, Stagecoach Mary, Bill Pickett, and Bass Reeves, these works have given me facts I never knew, told me stories I had never heard, and introduced me—through stunning photos—to many expressions of today's black cowboy culture. Though not a comprehensive list, many thanks to:

The Life and Adventures of Nat Love by Nat Love

Eight Seconds: Black Rodeo Culture by Ivan McClellan

Black Cowboys in the American West, edited by Bruce A. Glasrud and Michael N. Searles

Black Cowboys of Texas, edited by Sara R. Massey

The New Black West by Gabriela Hasbun

Black Rodeo in the Texas Gulf Coast Region by Demetrius W. Pearson

Black Cowboys of Rodeo by Keith Ryan Cartwright, with a foreword by Danny L. Glover

Juneteenth Rodeo by Sarah Bird, with an afterword by Demetrius W. Pearson

To my husband, Larry: Thank you for being my first reader. It matters more than you know. I love you.

To my daughter, Amina: Loving you is the most natural thing in the world. Thank you.

To Seneca Brand, a.k.a. Sha Love: What a blessing it has been to have you as a friend. I am so grateful for your generosity, support, and helpful notes.

To Carol Koonts: Your light is an inspiration. Thank you for being my friend and taking the most amazing author photos.

Thank you, Virginia Duncan, my editor, for your insight and trust in my work.

Thank you, Jennifer Carlson, my agent, for your steady guidance.

To the readers: You are the reason I get to do this. I am so blessed to be able to follow my heart and express myself through stories. Thank you for spending time with this one. I hope you've found something in these pages to hold on to.

And lastly, Texas—your wildflowers, sunshine, and big, blue skies will forever have my heart.